MW00711564

ONE

A Novel

SYDNEY JONES SERIES BOOK 3

Carolyn M. Bowen

One
A Novel

Copyright © 2020 by Carolyn M. Bowen

This book is a work of fiction. Names, characters, places, and incidents are the product of the author's imagination or are used fictitiously. Any resemblance to actual events, locales, or persons, living or dead, is coincidental.

The scanning, uploading, and/or distribution of this book without permission is theft of the author's intellectual property. If you would like permission to use material from the book, other than for review purposes, please contact Carolyn Bowen. Thank you for your support of authors' rights.

ISBN 978-1-7336858-4-9

ALSO BY CAROLYN M. BOWEN

FICTION
Cross-Ties
The Long Road Home
Primed for Revenge
Chance
Sydney Jones Series Books (1- 2)

NONFICTION
Cross-Stepping Your Way to Success

For Paisley Jane

CONTENTS

Prologue

THE WEATHER FORECAST was gloomy, and it was a dreary night in Georgia. One that wouldn't surprise you to see frogs parachuting from the sky head over tails. Sydney fell asleep listening to the pounding rain smacking the bronze roofing on an alcove above her bedroom window.

Spoiled from the architecture at her family's estate in Italy, her Italian father had designed the townhome to reflect the best of those features. The home was hers now, and she and her son David lived there.

She awoke at midnight groggy and sweating, consumed by a vision. She hadn't experienced a Native American dream state since recovering from her kidnapping, now ages ago.

Her mother's ethnicity appeared dominant in her looks and the ability to glimpse snapshots from the future. But with the melding of the Italian influence from her father's side and the golden bronze from her mothers, she was all their child in looks and heritage.

Afraid to move, to allow the video clip to continue playing before her eyes, she watched as the massive burnt orange rust infested shipping container dangled above her head. Held by ropes of iron chains, she saw it giveaway and the heavy dumpster crashed onto the top of her head, sinking into her skull. Shaken, and fearful of a premonition or an omen of evil, she wondered what it meant.

She slid her dark, well-shaped legs off the edge of the bed and touched her toes onto the soft contemporary Italian rug and set-up to reflect on the vision. Thinking swiftly, the orange color stood out in her mind, meaning danger or adventure, perhaps both. She didn't have time to sift through the ancient meanings her mother had shared. Nothing specific coming to mind, she went to shower and prepare for the day.

She forced herself to remember to smile in the mirror to bring happy thoughts to mind, for her son deserved a proper sendoff to school.

Her final case before leaving for vacation in Barbados was on the docket and needed her undivided attention. The timing couldn't be worse to have a premonition of evil towards her. She braced herself for the good morning ritual she and her son shared.

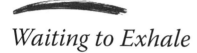

CHAPTER ONE

Waiting to Exhale

S YDNEY AND DAVID laughed and shoved the other away as they competed to be the first one to change the number on the chalkboard held by an angelic figurine sitting on their kitchen bar. They were counting down to their return to the island, the dream home Sydney bought in Barbados to vacation and be near her friends, and former nanny, Daniela and her husband Jonathan. The number they posted daily meant they were one day closer to living on island time for the summer. Today, David scrawled the number *ONE* on the board.

This was the crossover date, the last before their vacation. His school year ended, and her last case was on trial. She'd be glad for its conclusion, so she could relax with her son, David, and enjoy his school break for the summer.

They walked to the garage together. "Goodbye, David. I'll see you back home tonight after work." He turned his baseball cap around on his dark curly hair and waved as he pulled away in his Volvo.

Sydney dabbed on a fresh coat of peach-scented lip gloss before walking into the Fulton County courtroom in Atlanta to represent her client, Schupp Industries. Hans Renfroe, the company's CEO, was on her left wiping his sweaty palms on a monogrammed white handkerchief as the trial began. He wasn't smiling. The outcome could cost the business 1M plus with punitive damages on top of any compensatory damages award. In addition, the company could face government fines relating to safety in the workplace.

The company's argument was that the employee, Marc Jacobs, was careless in the machinery operation. The plaintiff's response was that it was an equipment malfunction. Jacobs himself described the accident. "I was operating the forklift to move flammable materials to the prep area when the forklift made a sudden dump. When the canister hit the concrete floor, it ignited on impact, throwing me 25' into the air."

Sydney countered producing records showing the recent satisfactory inspection of the equipment by OSHA. With information confirming Jacob's training on the use of the forklift by her private eye she added, "Training is mandatory for all employees who operate heavy equipment and machinery used in the plant."

On closer inspection, the firm's PI found the Schupp Industries hiring practices, in this case, didn't exist. They hired Marc Jacobs without the required certification and background check. He was friends with the floor manager, Joe Blankenship, and bypassed the mandatory basic qualifications. The good old boys' network was fully operational blindsiding her client and their efforts to win the case. She'd have a tough time convincing the jury with the evidence stacked against her client.

Sydney argued her client's equipment was in top working order when the accident occurred. She stated for the record, "All machinery and equipment have mandatory maintenance on a regular schedule." The documentation showing the forklift in question met the requirements and cleared for use was introduced as evidence. She said, "The accident resulted in human error—poor judgment by the plaintiff, Marc Jacobs."

During the court recess, she'd talked with her client, the president of the company, Hans Renfroe. "If they should call you to testify, don't refer to Jacobs as a dimwit, you can think it, but don't say it. The jury will wonder why you hired an unqualified person for the job leading back to your hiring practices. They'll assign blame to your company for not hiring qualified people with proper certification to do the job."

The jury was swift in handing down their verdict. The plaintiff didn't get his expected settlement. But they'd lost the case for the jury blamed the employer for substandard employee background checks and hiring practices.

Renfroe said, "They'll be a shakeup at the office when I return. Heads will roll, for company policies and procedures are in place to protect us and our employees. Here, the head of human resources will receive a reprimand, and the floor superintendent, Blankenship, will be fired immediately. We'll take unprecedented action to review our employee records, so we won't have a repeat of this."

"I'm sorry about how this turned out for you. Culpable damages and violations of code, and standards is a harsh response on top of the verdict."

"Trust me. We'll come out stronger with the changes I plan to make."

"I believe you will."

Sydney had one stop to make before driving home. She went into the office and left the paperwork for filing. She said goodbye to her office staff and managers. They wished her a relaxing vacation. As she maneuvered through the snarly traffic, her thoughts gravitated to life on the island. She could smell the fresh Caribbean salty air just thinking about it.

When she arrived home, she called out to David. His suitcase was sitting beside the front door, ready for their Uber pick up the following morning.

"I'm in here," he said.

She followed the sound of his voice. When she entered the kitchen, David was making a sandwich and smiled when she said, hello. "Well, I guess we won't order takeout, from the size of your sandwich. She laughed. I think I'll open a can of soup and have a salad. I'm too excited to eat much, anyway."

"Never stopped me," said David. He bit down on his mammoth sandwich, then wiped his lips before grabbing a handful of chips from the bag.

"I can't wait to talk face-to-face with Daniela, and look into her smiling eyes," she said. "We'll have them over for dinner often."

"Mom, not to hurt your feelings, but ask her to bring over the main dish, all right?"

"Well, David," she said. "What about my hiring a private chef for our stay?"

"Now, you're talking."

"I expect we'll be doing a lot of entertaining this summer. And I wouldn't want to botch our meals with my cooking." She laughed.

David shook his head and rolled his eyes. "I didn't mean to hurt your feelings."

"No problem, on the Chef's days off, we'll eat in town."

"That'll work!"

ooooo

Sydney glanced at the thermostat on the wall and lowered the temperature two degrees. At least their last night in Atlanta would be cool. Atlanta was a scorcher in the summer and set her mind at ease when referring to it as Hotlanta.

By this time tomorrow, she'd be sipping a cocktail on the terrace lounging beside the 45' infinity pool enjoying their Caribbean view. The cool trade breeze gently playing with the palm fringes, providing an island paradise awaited them.

She'd shipped ahead some personal items for her and David. An extra dermatologist prescribed sunscreen and her brand of toiletries, just in case they weren't available on the island. With his coloring, much like his father's, he'd be ebony by the end of summer. A conversational topic in Atlanta she'd accepted when questioned by nosy strangers about David's ethnicity.

When the alarm sounded the next morning, she awakened and touched the soft rug with her barefoot. She smiled, remembering their trip and quickly dressed before heading to the kitchen for coffee. A large box of Wheaties Cereal was sitting on the bar. David was already up and eating breakfast. He smiled when she entered and said, "You better eat, too. We have a long flight ahead of us."

"David, they serve meals on the plane."

"Yes, but I was starving after our last flight."

"Well, then have more cereal and fruit, we can't have you hungry again." She giggled acknowledging his herculean appetite and growth spurts were part of his becoming a young man.

ooooo

The Uber driver arrived and maneuvered them through the morning traffic and dropped them off at Hartsfield-Jackson International Airport. Their flight was an easy one, touching down on schedule at the Grantley Adams International Airport.

She hailed a taxi to drive them to their island estate called the *Dream Home*. Inside the garage, the new Porsche was waiting. Jonathan had collected it from the docks for her. The stiff tariffs and overseas transportation costs were nothing compared to the enjoyment she'd feel driving with the top down.

They arrived, and she tapped in her security code and slid the house key into the lock and opened the door. Their island home was exactly as they'd left it—inviting.

"David, I'll meet you on the terrace after unpacking my suitcase. How does a swim before dinner at Daniela's sound?"

"Great! I'll be down in a few."

She took the newly installed elevator to her bedroom suite to unpack her suitcase. David had taken the stairs two at a time, eager to dump his bag and change into his swimsuit.

In minutes, they met on the terrace. Sydney poured a glass of chardonnay from the bar and slid into a lounge chair to enjoy the Caribbean view overlooking the pool. David was swimming laps in the infinity pool.

After some time, she said, "David, it's time to go to dinner at Daniela's."

"Gosh, this felt so good. I've missed this in Atlanta."

"Just think, we have all summer to enjoy this."

She'd missed the Caribbean and other than weekend jaunts to the island because of David's youth sports, they didn't leave the city. This would change now that he was playing high school sports. No more summer youth leagues! But she'd done her part the way she thought Walker would have wanted. A natural athletic like his father, he needed a chance to gain confidence in his abilities. Now, he was a starter in football, and baseball for his high school teams.

Sydney popped the top of the Porsche, and they slipped into the new smelling car. The high-performance car hugged the road as she drove over to Daniela's. David said, "Wow, you're driving this stick shift like a pro."

"Well David, your mother may have hidden skills you're not aware of." She smiled.

Greeted with fanfare, Daniela hugged David and Sydney. The tantalizing scent of the Bajan seasoned seafood was overwhelming, making you want to lick the air to taste the special spices.

"I will get fat eating your cooking this summer," said David.

"Nah, it'll put meat on your bones," said Daniela. She laughed.

"We need a cook during our stay. Can you make a rec-ommendation?" asked Sydney.

"I do if it's tropical dishes you're interested in," said Daniela.

"With David's appetite and preference, it sounds like a great fit. And, the cook could live with us during our stay for convenience."

"I'll call my friends and get back to you."

"Thank you. I noticed the house next door to mine is for sale. Do you know anything about it?"

"The folks who retired there returned to the states to be close to family as they grew older."

Quickly thinking about previous attempts on her life, she said, "You know how much I value my privacy and the home is actually closer than I like a stranger living to us. I'll contact the real estate agent to view the property. Do you want to go with me?"

"Sounds like fun. I'm sure I'll drool over the ocean view."

Sydney and David said goodnight and returned home. Tomorrow he'd already booked a fishing trip on one of the island salt-water fishing charters. She planned to explore the island shops and meet Daniela to view the house next door.

CHAPTER TWO

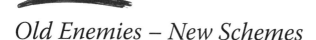

Old Enemies – New Schemes

JUDITH GARNER IS toasting her business accomplish-
ments in Puerto Vallarta Mexico with friends living
in her oceanfront community of expats. She'd been
buying, selling, and leasing properties to tourists and locals
alike. She planned to branch out to another island paradise
since it appeared to be her niche. The top destination in her
research was Barbados for its affordability, demand, English
speaking, and ties to the UK.

Excited about her new venture, she booked her flight and
accommodations at the Ivory Tower Hotel and Convention
Center. Tonight, was her send-off party for her extended stay
in Barbados to explore the possibilities and make her next
island investment.

On arrival, Judith realized the island would be income
producing for her. The airport was overflowing with tourists,
and the city streets were abuzz with shoppers and sightseers.

She went to a coffee shop in Bridgetown to sit, and people watch. She sat down at a table after ordering her flavored coffee. A tall, muscular man was standing at the counter and after ordering strolled over and sat beside a beautiful Barbadian woman.

Seeing him, Sydney's former bodyguard and head of security for her firm, Walker, came to mind. He looked different, but she'd recognize his confident stride anywhere. His makeover was mysterious. He had a secret, but what?

She left and met the real estate agent to view properties. From the oceanfront property, she saw a young man fishing from the next-door dock. He had Walker's build and old skin coloring, much darker than the man she'd seen earlier at the café.

As they were touring the luxurious house, Judith asked, "Who lives next door?"

The agent smiled and said, "Sydney Jones, the head of a prestigious Atlanta firm."

"I see, does she visit here often?"

"I don't know."

"Let's write up an offer for this home. I'd like to close as quickly as possible."

The sales agent leafed through her briefcase and pulled out an attorney's card saying, "Contact this office for lawyers, write all real estate agreements on the island."

"Consider it done."

"I'll wait to hear from your attorney and then welcome you to the island as a new homeowner."

Judith smiled. "Thank you for showing me around. I can't wait to hear from you again."

Judith took one last glance at the young man casting his line into the ocean and realized she'd found a bargaining chip for her next scheme.

There were some missing pieces to the puzzle. What was Walker doing with a woman at the café? Was he aware Sydney vacationed on the island with his son?

She'd do her research and plan the blackmail. She could feel it. There was money to gain from her new knowledge.

Back at the Tower's Hotel and Convention Center, she went to work. Yep, she'd found a new payday. She recognized Walker's photo in the obituaries from the AJC newspaper website. She wondered if Sydney knew he was alive for bribing her would bring a bigger payoff. Then she remembered their last conversation, and her saying, "I hope you rot in jail for stealing from and lying to me."

Well, blackmailing Sydney was out, but Walker was a different story. From the looks of things, he'd landed squarely on his feet.

Twirling her strawberry-blonde curls between her fingers and enjoying the scenery from high above the Caribbean in the hotel suite, she smiled. She was due to win against Sydney and Walker. Just when she could smell the money, her ole nemesis, Duane Nelson, came to mind.

Nelson was always at the forefront of her mind. He'd come to Mexico looking for her when his plans to marry and inherit from Sydney didn't work out. She'd fooled him into thinking she was broke after spending the money she's scammed from Sydney's investment accounts. Just as she'd done with the insurance company during her trial. No thanks to him for turning her into the law, hoping to score points with Sydney.

That time, she'd planned for his upheaval in her life. She'd moved from her oceanfront community to a neighborhood where she'd bought property to lease to locals when she realized he'd come looking for her with the payoff in mind. The one they'd concocted when his investigation leads him to her thievery. They'd made a deal. But they still charged her with wire fraud and theft. Had it not been for her smart attorney, she'd be in prison. Sydney's response to her plea for mercy still burned to the core. The insurance company paid her for the losses, but she refused to help.

She had the advantage, something she'd itched to have since last seeing them. Walker had no choice but to pay to keep his secret from Sydney and others interested in his whereabouts. The problem might force them to meet. She'd bet Sydney thought him dead after reading the news story. She was looking forward to the fireworks.

ooooo

Duane Nelson's funds were dwindling at his outback Montana hideout, where he operated his hunting expeditions for the big game. Using his funding from his days as a hired assassin, going by the anonymous name of Duncan in Atlanta, he'd left town just ahead of inquiries into his sideline business from his PI company. It was time to pay Judith Garner a visit, for although poverty-stricken when he last saw her, he'd bet she'd reinvented herself somehow, and she owed him.

Finding her latest address placed her living the high life in an Oceanside expat community in Puerto Vallarta. He planned his trip, for it was a pastime for payback.

When the plane touched down in Mexico, he went directly to her new abode. There was no answer to the doorbell chime and noticing a gardener trimming hedges, he asked where she was.

"Gone, he said. I heard she was vacationing in Barbados for a while."

"Do you know her address there?"

"I don't, but the Homeowners Association office might since she's friends and attends their events."

Duane thanked him and went in the direction the gardener suggested. A friend of hers at the HMO told him where she was staying in Barbados. He decided since he'd come this far, he may as well continue his pursuit and follow her there. Finding her home with her apparent busy schedule could prove difficult.

ooooo

Godwin watched on his computer monitor as his surveillance equipment recorded Duane Nelson leaving the airport in a rental car. He thought this was just like an old home week. The past was coming home to roost. First Sydney and his son, then Judith and now Duane. He wondered what plan for thievery they'd hatched up now.

He hated to tell Jenna they needed to cool it for a while. She needed to be a safe distance away from potential firepower directed at him or possibly Sydney.

She would not like it. Hell, neither did he. He made it a point to meet Alex, his charter fishing partner, and friend, to explain just in case Jenna complained to her cousin. They couldn't be painting the town for fear of running into his old nemesis. Until they boarded the plane leaving Barbados, he wasn't taking any chances, even with his complete makeover. Those two could blow his cover and have him back on the CIA's hit list or worst.

He made it a point to meet Alex and explain he had a business problem that needed his attention without distractions. He'd understand. Jenna required his full attention, and he knew it.

He met Alex at the docks, and he asked him to take two young kids out for their first deep-sea fishing trip. He'd given his deckhand the day off for family matters. The boys would need help to reel the big fish in and someone to cool down the reels while landing their catch.

Godwin said he'd be glad to help, for it was unlikely his tormentors would be on the ocean boating. When Alex told him the name for the charter, he almost choked. Sydney Jones had booked the charter for her son and his friend, from Alex's neighborhood.

This was his dream, to take his son fishing and teach him the ropes. The downside was that Sydney would drop her son off and return for him after the fishing trip. He needed to stay clear of her. He'd stay below in the captain's quarters while she was around and let Alex handle the rest.

Sydney arrived with David and she was beautiful as ever. He shook himself mentally when momentarily remembering their past. She didn't linger to talk with Alex, and it relieved him. He'd left the hatch open for fresh air and to listen from the cabin. When she left, he headed for the deck, then introduced himself to the boys.

"OK, guys pull aboard the fenders, the cushions that keep our boat from hitting the docks," he said. "And, we'll be off to our honey hole for the catch of the day."

"Aye, Aye, Sir," said David.

Alex coughed and said, "I think we've got a live one onboard."

"That's good, he'll need the strength to haul in the fish," said Godwin.

The seas were friendly as the boat rocked back and forth as they trolled past their fishing spot. The boys caught Bluefin and were robust in the handling of their fishing gear. Godwin smiled.

"Jim, I think you've met your match for reeling in the day's catch."

"Ah, or it's beginner's luck." He laughed and noticed the upturned lips of David.

"You think?"

"Well, it's settled. Another fishing trip is in our near future."

"You're on!"

They arrived back at the wharf in Bridgetown and Godwin cleaned the fish while David and his friend helped scrub the boat with a brush broom drenched in soapy water then rinsing with fresh water from the hose. He wrapped the fish up for David to take home for cooking. Sydney arrived within minutes after David called her. He went below until they were out-of-sight. He hoped his friend Alex didn't find his behavior unusual and ask questions.

After examining the vessel, they agreed it was spotless and ready for the next sea excursion. Godwin turned when leaving, remembering to thank him for inviting him to the charter.

ooooo

Relaxing in his lazy boy recliner after their fishing trip, his cell rang, and he answered it. He was clueless about how she found his number, but on the other end was Judith. In clipped succinct words, she said, "Meet me at the local coffee shop tomorrow at 10 a.m. I have something to discuss with you I think you'd like to hear."

He hesitated, then said, "I don't know who you are, but I enjoy meeting spunky ladies. I'll see you then."

He looked in the mirror and realized there was no way she could recognize him. If she thought she did, he had to convince her she had the wrong man. Otherwise, her vacation in Barbados would end early. He had too much invested in keeping his identity secret to let this opportunist jeopardize his life.

Meeting her would in the least inform him about her plans, and he'd bet they concerned Sydney too. He had to keep his thinking clear to manipulate her into disclosing her scheme. He'd bet it was a payoff she was expecting. If she thought he'd fall for blackmail, she was wrong. No one alive recognized his identity, and he planned to keep it that way.

They met. She stated he was Dan Walker. He politely listened while steam built up under his collar. She had a lot of nerve meeting on the assumption she would get a payoff for her silence. He wondered if she was packing a gun and would shoot him if he didn't agree. Then parlay his death into more for herself.

She talked about buying the house next door to Sydney and seeing his son fishing from the shore while viewing the property. He wondered if she planned to blackmail Sydney too. Was that the reason Duane Nelson had arrived at the island, he wondered. The two of them hatching plans together against Sydney and him?

He sat rigidly and under veiled eyes glared at her. She became more incensed when he didn't agree with her blackmail scheme. He kept Duane's presence to himself, for she might not be aware of his arrival.

Now he was hoping they weren't working together for knowing Judith she probably outsmarted him, and he could come for paybacks. When he laughed at her and said he felt sorry for the poor guy she was trying to blackmail, she lost it. She slammed her purse against the table and said, "You don't understand who you're messing with."

He said, "Yes, I do—a hungry little bitch."

She tossed her long curly strawberry blonde hair to the side and said, "You'll regret this!" Then she stormed out of the café without looking back.

He finished his coffee and made a mental note to find where she was staying. He'd bet Duane was there too, if not in the same room, close by.

ooooo

Judith went back to her hotel suite to think about her next move. A knock on the door caught her attention. She wondered if Walker, now known as Godwin, according to her real estate agent, had thought about her request and planned to pay her off. She unbolted the door and there stood Duane. He eased the door shut and locked it.

"I think it's time for you and me to have a little chat."

"I don't think so. I have nothing to say to you."

"Oh, but I think you do. You threw me off your tracks once when I found you in the Mexico slums, but not this time."

"Where are you stashing my money?"

"You don't have any, and I should never have agreed to pay you since it was your fault; they charged me with wire fraud and embezzlement."

"I saved your ass, even then. Who do you think ordered the kill on Maynard, the investment banker, and the prosecution's witness to your theft?"

"Yeah, right? You threw me to the dogs for your own benefit, to get closer to Sydney Jones. I am a self-made successful entrepreneur without the likes of you."

She was trying to keep calm, to think of something to make him go away. Should she tell him about Sydney and suspecting Jim Godwin was Walker. No. That was her gravy train, and he'd want to hijack it for himself.

Duane went to the kitchen and took an orange from a bowl to peel and eat. Apparently, she wasn't getting through to him. He wasn't getting anything from her. When he took out a blade from his pocket, he had her attention. She'd slipped by, not remembering how deadly he was. When he went by his alias Duncan, he usually contracted his hits. Yet, they'd had a close personal relationship, and he'd enjoyed their lovemaking. Maybe that would factor in for his next move.

He held up his knife from the peeling and said, "Judith, I will ask you one more time. Where's my money?"

She ran to the bedroom and quickly locked the door. Damn, she'd left her purse and cell in the living area. A blank cashier's check for buying real estate on the island was in there along with her passport showing her new identity.

In minutes, he said, "Judith Lambert, is it now? Well, this is a down payment for what you owe me."

"No way."

"Yes. I think it's time we settled. Either give me all my money or prepare for the consequences."

She searched for a way out of the bedroom. She'd gotten a penthouse suite and there was no way out except through.

Hidden behind the bedroom door, she said, "OK, calm down. I'm coming out, so we can find a solution. I've worked smart and hard for my money and don't plan to give you all. Perhaps we can come to an agreement."

"Now, we're talking. Come on out!"

She cracked the door marking his location, then skirted past him and took a seat on the luxurious sofa. "Sit down," she said. "And let's get done with your piracy."

He continued standing and said, "OK, what's your offer?"

"I'll pay you half-a-million to never see or hear from you again." In the back of her mind, she thought, I'll make this up and more from Walker and Sydney.

"OK, sweet cakes, here's your computer. Transfer it into my account now." Still standing, he handed her the laptop and walked behind the sofa to watch as she made the transaction.

She logged in to one of her banking institutions and asked for his account number. He pulled a slip of paper from his wallet and read off the routing number and his account number. He observed from behind her as she hit the send button and the confirmation popped up on the screen.

"Are you happy now?" she asked.

"Not as much as I will be."

He'd taken the knife from his pocket as she was entering the information. And when she turned to look at him with a smirk on her face, he reached over and slit her throat from ear to ear. The smirk on her face faded as the blood pulsated out of her neck. He smiled. Then he walked into the kitchen to clean his blade, turning on the faucet to run water over it before drying with a dishcloth. He then snapped it shut and shoved it into his jeans pocket.

Sidestepping the pool of blood forming beside her body, he rummaged through her suitcases for valuables. Filling one of her shopping bags with his findings, he added her purse and scattered notes from the coffee table before quickly logging into her computer and transferring a sizable deposit to his account. Shoving the computer in her go-bag for examination later was smart. Taking a small dishcloth, he wiped down the kitchen counter and his prints and eased the door closed with the heel of his shoe as he left.

His hotel room was a few feet away, and he quickly exited and was in his room changing his departure time and calling for a taxi for the trip home to Montana. The perfect spot for seclusion until the heat was off.

ooooo

When Judith didn't show up at the attorney's office to sign the paperwork to buy the home next door to Sydney's, they called her cell, then the hotel. The attendant said she'd not checked out. The attorney asked them to check on her, for she was to meet and sign some important papers. They politely requested a call back after talking with her.

A staff member took the elevator to her penthouse suite and knocked and said, "Hotel management. Could we have a minute?"

When there was no answer, he took his pass card and unlocked the door, and looked around while calling her name. Then he saw the puddle of blood and her lifeless body. He quickly called his manager and reported a murder. They informed him to secure the suite and return to the front office and call the police to investigate.

White-faced and trembling, he returned to his station and called the police to file a report, then the attorney's office as requested. He told him they had called the police to investigate her death. The attorney thanked him for the call and told him he was sorry and clueless about what may have happened.

ooooo

Walker worried about Judith's deductions and blackmail efforts. He'd found where she was staying and planned to end it forever. He was watching his surveillance of the airport and saw Duane leaving the island. A quick trip, he thought. He and Judith must have come to an agreement, or he'd still be poking around.

He noted someone had called the police to the Ivory Tower Hotel and Convention Center and wondered what happened. This was the hotel where Judith was staying. His first thoughts were Judith, and Duane had it out, and she lost. But if that happened, did she tell Duane about him and Sydney? He'd put money on Duane's early departure having something to do with the police's call to action. He'd wait. Duane might've done the dirty deed for him.

Now, if Sydney would get on a plane and return home, he could get back to his living his life and Jenna. He was sure Jenna was still pouting about his absence. But their relationship was friends with benefits – nothing more. He'd learned the lesson when the CIA ordered Isabella's murder and put him on a hit list. He'd not get close enough to any woman to put her in danger.

CHAPTER THREE

Moral Compass

S YDNEY WAS ENJOYING their Caribbean vacation. David had another growth spurt, and she was glad she'd packed a size larger for their stay. She saw Daniela often, and she and Jonathan came over to dine and swim in her pool. On one occasion, Daniela mentioned a faculty opening at the University. She said it would be great if they made Barbados their home year-round. The University had a great reputation, and she'd rock their law program. Sydney told her she'd consider her options, but reminded her she had a law office in Atlanta to return to. "But—few friends," said Daniela.

"You've got a point; I don't have many friends outside of work. I'll look into the possibilities, for I like the laid-back Caribbean lifestyle."

Sydney figured it would be impossible to make a career change now. Yet, it was an exciting thought. David was the happiest on the island with his new friends and their families. A man from the charter company, Godwin, had taken a special interest in him after their fishing trip. They went fishing at least once a week, along with David's fishing buddies. The boat captains had worked out a special deal for their charters—friends and family discount. David didn't think twice about asking to go deep-sea fishing often.

ooooo

Sydney kept up with local news and saw the headlines about a murder at the Ivory Tower Hotel and Convention Center. She remembered what Daniela had said on their first trip to the island. Locals didn't commit most of the crime, but criminals attracted to this tourist destination. She sighed. For living here this summer and meeting new people, she'd felt safe.

The follow-up to the news report said police found Judith Lambert from Puerto Vallarta, Mexico, murdered in her penthouse suite. She gasped when seeing the picture. The woman posted to the front of the news release was Judith Garner, her old impostor friend. She wondered what she was doing on the island and who murdered her?

Thoughts of Walker shrouded in the rock star Roxanne's murder came to mind. Although she felt he didn't do it, she'd always wanted to hear it from his lips. Now it was too late. He was dead.

ooooo

The possibility of teaching at the law school was tempting. Forwarding, her resume for consideration, would at least place her in the pool for guest lecturer during the summer.

And there might be a bright student interested in working at her firm in Atlanta.

The law school dean called and asked her to come in. She agreed. They met, and she talked about her interest and the demand for her time at the Atlanta office. But during the summer months, she'd love the opportunity to guest lecture. They agreed. She would lecture once a week during their stay on the island. She'd make sure David was well-cared for in her absence, either at a buddy's house or fishing with his friends on the *Eclipse* charter boat.

CHAPTER FOUR

Life Interrupted

G ODWIN WAS FOLLOWING the police investigation into Judith Lambert's murder. So far, there were no suspects. On the surface, the crime appeared to be from a random act of violence. She apparently opened the door for someone she was expecting without checking the identity of the visitor. The case was still under investigation.

The early report said the surveillance camera at her suite was malfunctioning, and there was no evidence collected. He almost wanted to tell them to check the outgoing flights for that day. But it would make many people suspect who was vacationing on the island.

He felt like he caught an extra breath, knowing she couldn't expose his identity. She was one less person to worry about. He just wondered if she told Duane. Time would tell, and the sooner the better. Jenna had given him an ultimatum, either to date her again or call it quits. And, to make matters worse, Alex agreed with her.

With Judith dead, and if Duane murdered her, he wouldn't return until it became a cold case. So why not give in to Jenna's wishes? He missed her female company. He called her and made a dinner date for the following evening at her favorite oceanfront restaurant.

ooooo

During their next deep-sea fishing trip, David proudly announced his mother would be a guest lecturer during the summer at the university law school. She was settling into the Caribbean way and although excited to spend time with David; he was ready for her to leave before something happened.

He kept an eye out for David on the days she taught. He was with a good bunch of boys, relatives of Daniela and Jonathan, and Alex. Yet, he paid attention for if Judith had seen David and him and made a connection, someone else could too. Duane came to mind.

ooooo

Duane was at his remote rustic retreat in Montana. He was stalling his next move until certain Judith's murder gave up no leads to him. Being cautious, he'd moved the stolen money to an offshore account and was waiting for signs he could return to Barbados to further his investigation about her findings.

Judith must have found a mother lode there from the notes he found in her hotel suite. Sydney summering in Barbados— hard to believe when she had multiple choices for the season.

And he doubted she'd spend the entire summer in one place with her options. Judith apparently thought it was valuable, or she'd told him rather than paying him off.

He'd wait out Judith's murder investigation, then pay a visit to Sydney's latest vacation spot. Knowing Judith had a nose for schemes, he didn't take her scribbling lightly.

ooooo

Sydney felt energized and more alive than she had in a long time. She was even darker now from enjoying her pool and oceanfront property. Her Native American heritage always made her skin tone appear to be golden, now a deeper, richer dark bronze.

Her long-time friend, Dominic Houser, often called and said he missed her. She told him the property next door is for sale and invited him to visit her and look it over. It would be a great spot to hideout when things got tough with his movie studio or one of his stars needed a getaway. Plus, he'd be next door to her. What could be better? He agreed. Before her return, he'd hop a flight to see her and check out this fabulous life she was living in the Caribbean.

Eager to have Dominic as a next-door neighbor, she called the property agent to get the details. The agent was the same one she'd used to buy her dream home. She told her owning the real estate might interest a friend. The agent confided all. She said the woman murdered at the Ivory Tower and Conference Center had put a bid on the house. Someone murdered her the day of its closing.

Sydney forced herself to breathe in and out. She recognized Judith Lambert as the thief and her former friend

Judith Garner. She asked, "What was the deciding point for Lambert making an offer?"

"When I told her – you lived next door. I didn't think it unusual. Everyone wants to live near the rich and famous."

"Consider the property sold. I'll contact my Barbados attorney and tell him to prepare the paperwork."

"Not a problem. I'm sorry I mentioned your name, but potential buyers, are always curious about next-door neighbors."

"No harm, done. By owning the property, I can keep it or sell to a friend."

She felt better after deciding and immediately call Dominic to let him know she owned the property now. He responded, "That's great for I just directed funds into a big production filming in our city. But perhaps I could rent it for business as needed."

"Sure, and you can always stay with us when you get a chance to get away."

"Thanks, I look forward to visiting your new haven."

Then she wondered what Judith Garner aka Judith Lambert was doing in Barbados surely, she didn't think they could be friends again. Knowing Judith, she was scheming, but to what end?

CHAPTER FIVE

Thin Line

SYDNEY MET JIM Godwin officially when she picked up David and his friend, Jason, from their fishing trip. Oddly, she felt his presence the first time she dropped off her son for the charter. She remembered the same sensation when seeing a broad-shouldered man sitting on the groom's side at Daniela's wedding. Could he be the same man and if so, what was their connection?

Godwin was cordial and complimented her son, David, for his behavior and fishing skills. Alex the charter captain laughed and said, "Finally someone to give Jim some fishing competition."

She was glad they had fun and would like to learn more about Jim Godwin. It relieved her they'd cleaned the fish. David asked, "Mom, how about inviting everyone over for dinner tonight? I bet Jim would be glad to show you how to cook them."

Everyone turned and looked at her, and she said, "Good idea, David. Some help to prepare and cook the fish will be welcome. You're all invited to our house for dinner tonight. Bring your swimsuits to enjoy the pool."

David's friend, Jason, chimed in, "Great!"

She looked at Jim and Alex and said, "You, too, and bring a friend if you'd like."

Jim said, "I'll come over early to help cook the fish. Thanks for inviting me. Alex, are you coming?"

"No, sorry, I've already made plans. But next time."

ooooo

Godwin brought seafood seasoning for the fish from the local herb and produce market. He rang the doorbell and in minutes Sydney opened the door and invited him in.

"Welcome to our home," she said.

"Thanks for inviting me."

"I appreciate your coming early to prepare our dinner. I have almost zero Barbadian culinary skills and do not understand how to prepare and cook fresh fish, much to my son's disappointment."

He looked around while thinking his place was nice, but hers was over the top. She led him to the commercial-grade kitchen after he handed her a triple distilled and aged bottle of Mount Gilboa Rum - Barbados. A bold rum suitable for her personality, he thought.

"Make yourself at home," she said.

Ahh, how he wished he could. If she could read his mind, she'd be shocked to learn his difficulty in keeping his hands off her. Underneath the facade, he was still Walker.

"Thank you, your kitchen is top-chef quality."

"Yes, perhaps if I'd learned how to operate the appliances." She laughed. "No kidding," she said after he gave her a surprised look like he didn't believe her.

He quickly found a sharp knife and a large Tupperware marinating container to begin the process. Gutting the Wahoo at the wharf before bagging them saved time and a mess to clean up.

Using Alex's native recipe, he prepared the Wahoo with Bajan seasoning using fragrant lime-spiked garlic, chive and onion puree skipping the scot pepper for David's palate. He then set the Wahoo aside to marinate no longer than 45 minutes before grilling. He didn't want the acidity in the lime to alter the texture of the meat.

Sydney mixed them a drink and one thing certain she'd learned Barbadian style bartending. He thanked her and took a sip of the perfectly made rum cocktail.

Being around Sydney he had to check himself to keep from giving her a loving embrace or playfully kiss the tip of her nose, the norm when they were together. Jenna would have a fit if she realized their background and his being here tonight. How far he could take the friends with benefits thing with her, he did not understand. For certain, no one would stand between him and his son, even if he couldn't claim him. And Sydney—always and forever in his heart!

After seasoning the fish, he began making the side dishes of pigeon peas and rice, and stuffed avocados with Sydney's help to make David's favorite—macaroni pie. They had dinner covered with Daniela bringing a pineapple pie for dessert.

Their guests arrived. Daniela and Jonathan followed by David's friend and parents. The boys already wearing swimsuits headed for the pool. The adults gathered around the island bar on the terrace as Sydney pours drinks, much to everyone's satisfaction. After a brief conversation, he placed the fish on the grill for in minutes dinner was ready. They dined on the terrace overlooking the Caribbean.

After everyone left, Walker stayed to help clean-up. Every minute in Sydney's presence counted toward a future memory like a breath of fresh air. She rejuvenated his soul.

When ready to leave for home, he said, "Good night." David walked over and hugged him and said, "Thanks for cooking dinner, it was great."

Behind him, he saw Sydney teary-eyed and reached for her hand. Pulling her closer in her scent and memories captivated him from long ago.

ooooo

Duane Nelson was stalling for time, waiting for the manhunt to be over for Garner's killer before returning to the crime scene. Judith was on to a big payday she'd discovered there. He wished now he'd extracted the latest scheme before killing her. She was too quick to transfer money into his offshore bank account. A backup plan was in place, and he needed to retrace her steps from the time she landed to uncover the mystery.

He had gone through the notes she'd scribbled, trying to piece together the puzzle. She'd tucked the napkin in her purse with an initial followed by a question mark. Who was the *W* she met at a local café? He'd follow the lead. She was buying a home on the island. The band draft in her purse identified the sales agent. That would be a start. He could talk to the agent while acting interested in buying property.

From his news sources, he felt it safe to make the return flight to Barbados. The police had gotten nowhere in their investigation into her murder. With no family or close friends, there was no pressure to find her killer. This benefited him. Finding Judith's murderer was likely a cold case by now. He booked his flight.

ooooo

Godwin was at his computer monitoring happy vacationers, mostly as they disembarked from the airport. He'd programmed likely enemies into his surveillance app for alerts when entering the island. The hair rose on the back of his neck when he saw Nelson with his baseball cap partially camouflaging his face get into a taxi. He wondered what he was up to, for he'd stake his last dime he was Judith's killer. Why would he return to the crime scene? Greed. Nelson knows something.

He was glad his and Jenna's relationship played out. For he couldn't go to any of the places she'd want to go right now. He'd spent time with his son on the boat and grilling dinners at Sydney's home. So close, but still untouchable. He couldn't put her in the crosshairs again. He lived for the moments they could be together as a family, if only in his dreams.

Identifying Nelson's whereabouts was daunting, for it was unlikely he'd return to the Towers Hotel and Convention Center—the scene of the crime. The Montana outback game hunter could hunker down almost anywhere, likely a cheap hotel near the airport for a quick getaway. Narrowing his search for a likely spot for someone on the run, he found him at a no-frills lodge.

If it wasn't for his damn burner phone, he'd monitor his activities closer. He bypassed his morning ritual and went to the coffee shop where he'd met Judith. If Duane was on to him, he'd make a visit there to retrace Judith's steps.

He'd no sooner ordered his cup of coffee when through the door strolled Nelson. Just as expected, he didn't have the answers but was searching for them. He'd killed Judith before learning her secrets and was scrapping for details from what she left behind to discover her plan.

Before leaving home for the cafe, he gazed into the mirror to convince himself he was unrecognizable as Walker. Now, he could play a cat-and-mouse game with him. The dead giveaway to Garner had been his height and bulk. This time would be different for he'd not stand but sit back, relax, and listen.

Here we go again, he thought. A real estate agent came in and waved at him. He nodded in reply and said, "Good morning."

She ordered her cappuccino and went to the table where Duane sat. He listened. He overheard Nelson asking if 4505 Hawthorne Pass was still on the market, the home next door to Sydney. When the agent said, "No, it sold to the next-door neighbor, Sydney Jones. But we have other luxury homes near this one."

"I, see," he said. "I wanted to learn more about that one for its location and waterfront amenities. Do you think she'll sell?"

"That's not likely. She's very peculiar about her next-door neighbors. If it sells, it'll be to her friends."

"Too—bad, for I'd marked that waterfront home on my computer back home before my trip. Do you think we can take a drive out there and I'll show you what I like about the home?"

"I see no harm in that. When we finish our coffee, I can show you around, but only from the outside for its private property now. Tell me what attracts you to this home and I'll show you one with those advantages."

"Sounds reasonable."

∘∘∘∘∘

Walker sipped his coffee, thinking whatever Duane is looking for relates to Sydney, damn. To make matters worse, David will probably fish from the shore when he arrives. He quickly calls him to invite him deep-sea fishing. "Just get your mother to drop you off at the wharf. I'll meet you there."

"Sure, see you in a few."

One bullet dodged, for David was the spitting image of him, the old Walker. He didn't want Duane to uncover anything more than he already suspected. He'd bet he was looking for something to blackmail Sydney with, which was the direction Judith headed when he snuffed her out.

They had a fun day fishing and caught grouper for the evening meal. They cleaned the fish at the dock, and he drove David home, and said, "See you later, this evening."

"Sure, man."

He'd need to be careful in case Duane was staking out her place. He rode his motorcycle where he could hide it from street view. One thing he knew—Sydney enjoyed his cooking. And, she'd not once associated his Caribbean cooking with the dishes Walker once made in her Atlanta home. Her grief was ever-present from his sudden death. He could see the sadness in her eyes. The least he could do was give her the night off to enjoy the cool ocean breeze while he grilled. Ahh, he wished for more.

ooooo

Duane was coming up empty-handed. Whatever Judith was plotting was unclear to him. Being no dummy, he recognized Sydney Jones was involved. Otherwise, why would she agree to buy the luxury home next-door?

He had an itch he couldn't scratch. Back when he was running his Duncan enterprise, he could salivate and take on kills for hire himself instead of contracting the hits with his fellow sojourners. He missed those days. And, no thanks to Sydney Jones, he was out of a business clearing town ahead of the law enforcement. He wanted something or someone to blow up. He loved firing off explosives—sort of his go-to strategy to suit the purpose. And he'd love to blow Sydney off the face of the earth. He'd bet there was a killing contract somewhere on the dark web, just for that very thing. He boarded his flight home and pondered his next move, for he'd not press his luck targeting her in Barbados.

Godwin observed Duane leaving Barbados on his surveillance equipment. He sighed, hoping that meant he'd found nothing. Otherwise, he'd still be poking around. Popping the top of a beer, he relaxed, looking forward to the evening with David and Sydney - his family.

CHAPTER SIX

Murderous Intent

T HE SUMMER WENT by in a flash and Sydney and David
       returned home to Atlanta on the day before her leave of
       absence from the firm ended. She was aware he'd miss
his new friends and it would be some time before they could
return. She had much work to do and a new attorney from
Barbados to introduce to her partners and staff.

The early morning ritual began immediately. Sydney got
up and dressed early for her morning commute to work. David
was already sitting and having breakfast in the kitchen when
she got downstairs. She said, "Good morning, I see you're
ready for school. Are you stopping by your friend, Stefan's
house to pick him up on your way?"

"Yes, I called him last night, and we made plans today
for after school. "I'll pick him up and after our ball practice
drop him off."

"OK, drive safe and text me when you get home."

"Mom, it's not like you bought me a sports car, like yours to drive. My Volvo is a steady ride and gets me from A to B. I don't think anyone will want to race me." He laughed.

"Laugh if you want, but I feel better knowing you're driving a heavy-duty car."

"I know Mom. Have a great day back at work." He grabbed his gym bag and kissed her on the cheek before leaving.

"I love you," she called out. He turned and smiled, and said, "I love you too, Mom."

Sydney hurriedly gathered her purse and locked the doors. She was driving her Porsche with the top down and planned to beat the rush hour traffic to her downtown office. Driving when the highway was wide open and not bumper to bumper was fun and a relaxing way to begin the day. And, she was looking forward to meeting Deputy Director Thomason at the coffee shop where they regularly met. She'd bet he was only a few car links behind her now, pushing his so-called sterile-looking government vehicle to the max.

She was singing along with her forever favorite singer, *Whitney Houston*, singing *I'll Always Love You* when a motorcycle came out of nowhere and kept pace along the empty highway. When she slowed, the biker did the same. She felt like flipping him, off–the dummy. Just when she thought the heck with getting a ticket and was ready to floor it, she realized a grenade had been thrown into her car. She saw the biker pull in front of her and accelerate at full throttle and then...

The last thing Sydney remembered was the smile on her son's face as he left home. When her car exploded, she was blown out ending up face down on the highway, or that's what she'd heard the nurse say at the change of her shift to the new attendee.

The pain of recovering from a near-fatal crash and being identified as a Jane Doe usurped her energy. There was one thing keeping her going–her son. But, no one was aware of her agony. She couldn't speak or even raise her arms. When the raw pain from the injuries became unbearable, she succumbed to the darkness and faded into a medicated abyss.

ooooo

Her friend, Deputy Director Thomason visited every day. He waited patiently for her to regain consciousness. If she survived this attack, she needed a new identity, one without a target on her back. And he was just the man to create her new image. She'd confided her background and family ties to Italy that had made her father's restaurants famous. Now, that she'd followed through with their exit strategy from long ago, he could move faster–and time was of the essence.

Sydney had laughed and made jokes about her exit plan when she handed him the envelope with the details in the event, she couldn't carry them out herself. He left it unopened until the morning of her car crash. A brief note inside explained her wishes and plans for David if she couldn't take care of him. He read her handwritten words and tears filled his eyes knowing she put her son's wellbeing first.

When this was all said and done–meet Gabrielle. Flush with the money she'd moved from her bank accounts without a trace for worst-case circumstances. He was glad she'd carried out their plan for he'd known things could get bloody with the criminal cases she represented and the people she angered in general when advocating human rights.

He left an Italian audible of a romance novel by her bedside to help her make the transition. She was once fluent in the language for her father never departed from his roots. He wanted to remind her so when she surfaced from the trauma, she'd be speaking the language and hopefully with an accent.

He'd already told Daniela to expect an aunt from Italy to take over the care of David. She was distraught from learning of Sydney's death and barely made it through the memorial service to comfort David. The last of Sydney's immediate family to be killed in a suspicious accident was traumatic. He was determined to buy her time to heal before taking her place beside her son.

The lies he was prepared to tell on her behalf were endless. When they had concocted the plan for Sydney's new identity, she laughed and said she had nine lives like the tomcat, named Tommy, she had growing up. Now, he was glad she'd followed through and changed her investments into her new name. The income was paying for her lengthy and expensive stay in the private burn unit.

How things turn out depended on what she remembered—and his swaying her to his beliefs. Once. Twice. Three times she'd dodged a bullet. He hoped she remembered their planning her exit from the legal world. So far, everything had gone well with faking her death. But, to look at her you'd never recognize it was Sydney. She laid there with scabs covering much of her body, pus oozing although the bandages were replaced often. She'd need cosmetic surgery before meeting her son again. There would be no doubt she was a burn victim otherwise and raise questions about her identity. Dear God, he prayed...

CHAPTER SEVEN

Dark Shadows

H IS AGENCY WAS investigating the links to her car bombing. Cross-referencing her personal caseload with possible murderers seeking revenge. Political pressure was directed at him to find her killer quickly. He didn't need an incentive. They were friends and that was enough. They'd find the bomber and not miss a detail. For whoever was behind this would be brought to justice.

He was scrolling through pages on his computer screen recapping Sydney's cases looking for potential leads. She'd tried many cases that could cause her grief. From human trafficking to industrial sabotage, and personal injury all were of significant impact with repercussions for dangerous outcomes.

But—who lobbed the grenade into her Porsche convertible during that fateful early morning commute? He briefly recalled her run-ends with the Beijing group, but the case would be tied up in court for a long time with the U.S. and

China wrestling over dominance. They'd wanted to scare Sydney into taking their case, not kill her, at least not then.

He read through her human trafficking case files and would've been shocked at the villains named if not in law enforcement. There was potential for fallout from any one of them. He ranked the contenders on his file to investigate further.

After reviewing her court cases, he decided to look more into her personal life. For a while, it had been messy, and she'd gotten involved with some unscrupulous people who she considered friends. But, when she learned who her real friends were, she ditched the impostors.

There was always something off about the PI, Duane Nelson. He couldn't put his finger on exactly what, but Sydney broke-off all contact with him. He'd check his current location and follow up on Judith Garner's whereabouts. He'd give Special Agent Manning his notes for follow-through while he was away from the office.

Every day he went by the burn care center where he'd hidden Sydney. Some days were better when she was in less pain. Still unrecognizable, she'd have the facial reconstruction surgery when her condition stabilized. He'd contacted the best surgeon in the south knowing Sydney would have wanted special care.

Looking over her chart, the doctor scheduled the surgery three months out depending on her medical condition. For the severe injuries to her face, was jeopardizing a complete recovery and the likelihood of breathing on her own. Pleased with his prognosis, he told the cosmetic surgeon, Dr. Lyons to make her look like a movie star, and showed him a picture of the passport photo she'd purposely chosen for her new identity as Gabrielle D'Agostino.

He couldn't wait for the bandages to come off and have one less medical and identity problem to worry about. He'd put her credit card on file for her medical attention at the burn clinic. He checked it daily to see the expenses piling up and being paid for her care.

He couldn't believe his good fortune in being the first one to the crime scene. They'd planned to have a coffee at a shop near her office. And, he was on the way there when he received the call on GA 400 when he was en route for meeting her there from home.

For he and Sydney had planned for the worst-case scenario with her having a fake identity, her will written, provisions for her son, and assets transferred upon her death. He liked the name she chose – Gabrielle D'Agostino. He loved the way it rolled off his tongue. She'd laughed and said, "It sounds very Italian!" He'd love to see her laugh again. Today wasn't that day.

He sat by her bedside and started reading from a poetry book he'd picked up from the bookstore nearby. Most nights, unless working, he stayed in the oversized recliner next to her and slept in fitful sleep dozing at times yet always aware of where he was. He wanted to be with her in case she became conscious and was afraid.

She hadn't missed a step after making plans for her and David's future. He just didn't expect her to be blown up. He could still see her waving the power of attorney she'd prepared in the air while mouthing the word freedom. Neither of them had expected this catastrophic departure when exiting her past identity.

He had Special Agent Manning checking with the Department of Transportation to get the footage from GA 400 around the time her car was bombed. He hoped it was an eye-opener for arresting the culprit who destroyed Sydney's life. She was dead to her past. And, with her body incinerated in the fiery crash according to his report, the assassin would be charged with murder.

Sydney's eyelids twitched, and he stood and slowly approached her bedside and whispered Gabrielle... With tubes running in and out of her body, she looked the part of what happened to her – blown up. The ventilator keeping her alive was making melodic beats with a slight hiss, then returned to its cadence. He carefully touched her bed and spoke softly assuring her she was being cared for by the best. He pressed the nurse call button and in minutes the room was filled with the medical team.

"Gabrielle, can you hear me?" the physician asked. "Blink your eyes if you understand."

She blinked her eyes and the doctor said, "I think we can begin removing your ventilator. We'll take it slow, tell me when you're in pain, and we'll wait a minute before resuming."

Tears formed at the corner of her eyes, Gabrielle blinked again and pointed toward the tube down her throat. He said, "I gotcha. I think we can remove it now."

The nurse filled a cup with water from the bedside stand and held it for her to sip through the straw. Daily the staff had freshened her room for the day she'd awaken. Gabby made eye contact with him, and he caught himself before bursting into tears. He stepped back giving the medical team time to evaluate her condition and to get his emotions under control.

When the medical team was satisfied, she was doing well on her own, they packed up their equipment and left. She now looked almost human with bandaging around her face and salves covering her bodily burns. He decided to stay with her. She needed a chance to get reacquainted with her situation. There was also a possibility she may have seen her assassin. He had some personal leave time coming and today it was needed.

She slept and he texted the agent-in-charge to see if he'd gotten the video footage from the DOT. He texted back they were viewing it now. Thomason smiled, and texted-tell me what you find. Will do, was the swift reply.

Gabby slept most of the day, and he realized that was part of the healing process. The sooner the better. He needed to get her out of town to continue her healing until she was ready to meet her son and return to her dream home in Barbados.

He'd considered taking her to his home for the interim, so he could be close by if needed. Yet, he didn't want to do anything that could arouse suspicion about her. When she became stable, he'd fly to Tuscany with her to a family home she'd left for Gabrielle as another escape route. She'd mentioned the possibility when setting up her new identity as Sydney's aunt.

Neither of them foresaw the horrific event she'd suffered. He was glad she'd made plans for her son in case of her death, and financial means to support him and the new Gabrielle D'Agostino. He hoped Daniela wouldn't question, her aunt's delay in coming to Barbados after the funeral. He had to stop himself from overthinking. She still had a long way to go before being cleared by her doctors for release from the burn unit.

CHAPTER EIGHT

Blue Skies

DUANE NELSON HAD gotten enough of Atlanta and returned to his rustic hideaway in Montana. He was Chilin', kicked back and relaxed enjoying the coolness the mountains provided in the autumn. He had plenty of canned goods and fresh Elk meat hanging in his smokehouse to last through the winter.

He was watching his favorite shows, reruns of the Law and Order series which was about all he could pick up from his remote cabin. He now had a hotspot for using his phone to keep up with newsworthy topics, most importantly, a manhunt for him.

Sometimes he still wondered what Judith Garner was up to in Barbados. He figured a payday for some scheme she'd planned. But he wasn't going to dwell on it, for now, he had all her money transferred into his account using her laptop and then destroyed the evidence. He'd not be pinned for that cons murder. He decided it was time to go down the mountain to the pub in the small town. When desired he picked up female companionship for a night on the town and an evening at the two-star hotel next door.

ooooo

After Sydney's memorial service, Daniela and Jonathan settled into her dream home on the bottom level leaving David with his suite next to his mother's upstairs. When Sydney's aunt, Gabrielle arrived they'd move next door to the oceanfront property Sydney deeded them. When they sold their house, they stored their furnishings there along with what the previous owner had left behind. Jonathan had set up his office there away from the noise of David and his friends frolicking in the pool or playing games in the media room.

Godwin was David's constant companion and came over regularly for dinner and a swim. He was teaching him about captaining a charter boat for they both loved fishing. They'd bring their fresh catch home often and they'd cook and eat every morsel.

David was doing well in school, especially under the circumstances. Having friends on the island helped him slowly grieve for his mother. He'd make it for the community supported him and Godwin was always a phone call away.

David was growing and she'd begun ordering his clothes online to get his extra-large and tall sizes. When he and Godwin were out and about, they looked related, both tall and bulky. Daniela wasn't surprised he enjoyed playing basketball with the other boys his age. He was smart and athletic; his mother would be proud of him.

CHAPTER NINE

The Fight for Forever

GODWIN WAS STILL tracking leads in the murder of Sydney. Scrolling the darknet he'd found a hit posted on her in Atlanta shortly after her return from the island. Looking further he noted the employer took pains to hide his/her identity. The ISP bounced like a beach ball across cities in the U.S. to Beijing. What was the missing piece of the puzzle, he wondered?

Her killer was likely linked to her past affiliation with the Chinese Nationals she'd represented for a time then refused further cases. Intrigued for he thought that chapter had played out with his ending Ming Chang's revenge on Sydney. Being mindful he was dealing with a computer ace he pushed deeper to find the identity of the contractor. The name Chang Bohai, came forward, the son and inheritor of Ming Chang and her husband's huge financial reservoir.

He was living and attending a University in the United States when he ended Ming's vengeance. Knowing her, she probably left a note with her legal representative for him, pointing to Sydney, a woman who tried to rob her of what was rightfully hers with her relationship with her husband's mistress, Nancy Lynn.

He sensed the clock was ticking to locate the hitman and end his killing rampage. Hiding his identity, he dove deeper until he dug out the photo of her burning vehicle and transfer of money to an assassin with the handle, Duncan. Yep, he recognized the name from early in his protection detail for Sydney. None other than the two-faced PI Duane Nelson. He wondered if Thomason was aware. If not, he would for he'd not stop until he did.

ooooo

With the help of David, who'd proven to be a gifted computer scientist already, they'd tested a new technology app to protect websites from being hacked. After BETA testing, he sold the app to a computer technology company for a hefty figure. He paid David, some immediately for his help getting the app market-ready.

He opened Barbados's savings account for David with substantial dividends from the sale. He suggested technology might be a good career path for him. He was always interested in what he was working on for his technology clients and he showed him the ropes. When not in school they were trying out new tech ideas and saltwater fishing.

ooooo

Months had passed...

Sydney slowly recovered and Thomason was anxious to get her out of the states to her home in Tuscany far away from

Atlanta. His agent had done a great job of securing the footage from Sydney's car bombing and with laser-precision identified her killer as Duane Nelson. He'd relayed the information to all law enforcement agencies to proceed with caution for he was armed and dangerous.

Within days, he'd check her out of the hospital for their direct flight to Tuscany. He'd saved up leave time, not having a family to vacation with, and now he had five weeks of vacation at his disposal. He'd already booked their flight going on the date the doctors predicted her release.

He'd planned for their drop-off at the airport by Uber. He'd packed his suitcase and brought Gabby a few changes in clothes from her townhome. He'd slipped in late at night to get her personal items and toiletries, and packed her bags for the transcontinental flight. Then he erased his presence from the security camera footage. Soon the doctors would sign-off, and they'd be on their way, untraceable, out of the country–finally.

He smiled and realized Gabby was getting better when she complained about the hospital's dietary restrictions. She'd ate enough Jell-O to last a lifetime, she said. Antsy to be reunited with her son, she was ready to go.

He figured the doctors would release her today. Although she'd be left with some scarring, if she followed their directives she'd mend at home. He'd given notice of his vacation leave to coincide with the timing of her release and was ready to escort her out of Atlanta.

ooooo

Duane was passing the time playing the market with his new-found money. He'd placed a ceiling for how much he'd spend day trading, not being certain of the outcome. He was ready to take over Judith's Puerto Vallarta residence as a long-lost uncle, her only kinfolk. He needed an escape route in case things got tight in the states.

He had downloaded the description of the property and with a few keystrokes deeded the property to himself using the signature she'd stored on her computer for transactions in Barbados before trashing her computer. He figured he'd hold-up in Montana until the freeze then vacates for the warmer climate.

The isolation of his cabin was nice when the heat was on, but he was beginning to feel claustrophobic. There was no news about Judith's death in Barbados and Sydney Jones was a clean sweep leaving nothing but fragments of her sports car behind. He booked his flight to Mexico and decided to go down the mountain one last night to the bar he frequented for a social outlet. Little did they know, but it would be a long time before he returned—if ever.

He cranked his old CJ-7 and embarked on his final night of drinking and whoring until he found suitable replacements in Mexico. Ever who the lucky girl was tonight, he'd screw her until he was fulfilled—at least for a short spell.

He parked in the next-door hotel parking lot knowing that'll be where he ended up and made reservations for the night. Then, he walked next door to the bar. He recognized some of the regulars and gave a curt nod in their direction when they looked his way. The barkeep stocked his brand and within minutes his bourbon was served. Nothing but the best, Crown Royal Bourbon Mash and he suspected the owner stocked plenty of the Canadian whiskey for his occasional visits, and for his supply when returning home.

Damn, he may as well be drinking at home. No one was talking and there were no women in the bar. But it was early yet as he always hooked up with a prostitute when he came down the mountain. Tonight, would be no different, he thought mentally calculating the timing of past visits. He sat on the bark bar stool with an elk hide cushion and initials and symbols carved into the handles and waited. This place was too damn quiet for him. He strode over to the jukebox and dropped some quarters in to play some music. He shrugged his shoulders for the music made him want to dance. Where were the women?

Within minutes the place was swarming with the local law enforcement. He'd pinpointed the employees' only backdoor for it was his job to locate all the exits as a private investigator. He headed toward the restroom and exited quickly through the kitchen. His hotel room was next door booked under an alias with his room facing away from the bar. He sped up his walking pace until he was safely behind the closed door.

He'd like to understand what was happening. Apparently, the barkeep was in on it, for someone alerted the women not to show. Could he trust him to give a straight answer about who they were expecting to find? He'd check him out in the morning, then he was leaving town after a quick stop at his cabin to pick up his new passport and luggage.

He looked out his hotel window and saw the cop cars leaving and recognized he needed to blow this town. For even if they weren't looking for him, he didn't like them around.

He'd find out first thing in the morning, who they were looking to knab.

He had the continental breakfast in the hotel's small break room if you could call coffee and a cinnamon swirl breakfast. Then strode around the building to Guthrie's Bar next door.

He was in luck for the owner was in perhaps because he'd closed the bar early last night after the law enforcement raid. The regulars vacated the place not wanting to be a part of whatever was going down. He took his usual barstool and the bartender poured his drink and set it down on the cleanly wiped still damp Brunswick bar counter. He took hold of the bourbon glass and looked around before speaking. "By the way," he said. "Why was the law enforcement here last night?"

"They were looking for a suspect in a murder," he said.

"You don't say."

"Yep, they want this guy bad."

"Did they get him?"

"No, but they will, every law enforcement agency in the states are looking for him."

"Did they happen to mention a name in case I've run into him?"

"Yep, there looking for Duane Nelson. He murdered a woman in Atlanta."

"Don't recognize the name."

"Didn't figure you would since you hold up in your cabin most of the year."

"You've got that right."

Duane finished his drink and said good-bye and walked back to the hotel to his jeep. For he'd not brought anything with him down the mountain so no need to return to his room. He was ready to gather his suitcase from the cabin and catch his flight before law enforcement caught up with him.

Getting through security at the main airport could be a bitch. He'd booked his flight from Bozeman a little over 30 miles away from his cabin to Puerto Vallarta Mexico. He was proud of his foresight of booking earlier and applying for a Transportation Security Administration, TSA status, before his Barbados trip. He finessed his way through the interview and now there'd be less screening at the airport, the better for his getaway.

After arriving at the airport, he was relieved to learn his flight would be on time. He was one of the first through the gate to take his first-class seat for the over 8-hour flight to Gustavo Diaz Ordaz International Airport (PVR). After settling in, his thoughts went back to how law enforcement got a lead on him in Montana.

He'd kept his identity secret and had gone by an alias since leaving Atlanta the first time after Sydney figured out his scheme. The only thing he could figure was the night he got exceptionally drunk and was overly physical with a call girl he'd met at the bar. Did she take a photo of him with her cell after he passed out drunk and alerted the cops?

Damn, he couldn't even remember her name, and barely recalled her except she'd demanded cash upfront. She'd better be glad he was moving on and would never see her again. One of the old faulty wells at the cabin would make a perfect dump for her body. He smiled, thinking he always had the answers.

ooooo

The owner of Guthrie's Bar went about his usual stocking of liquors glad law enforcement had moved on so his regulars would return for drinks, conversation, and women. He'd alerted the women of the night, not to come during the raid by mentioning it to Candy. She'd tell the other women for they stuck together.

Candy had alerted him to a problem when she shared a photo of herself after Duane had beaten her. She'd taken a photo of him when he passed out to show the other women what a monster he was and to warn them about him. Afraid, to return to the bar, she'd come in early one morning, and told him what happened. He asked his friend at the Sheriff's office to run his photo figuring he was on the lam from something hiding out at his cabin for the most part. That was when they'd gotten a hit and found he was a suspect in an Atlanta murder.

Duane had seen the sheriff's car through the tinted and smoke clouded bar windows and slithered out the backdoor like a snake into the night. He figured he was gone back up the mountain to escape capture and was surprised the next morning when he showed up. Undoubtedly, he wasn't aware he was a murder suspect or was brave as hell, maybe both. Either way, he delivered the message he wanted him to hear, he was wanted, and the law was on his trail. That should be enough to make him vacate the Rockies and never return. He was quite pleased with the way things turned out. He'd be caught sooner or later, and their small town would've sidestepped the notoriety of harboring a murderer. A decisive win for his business and the local economy.

CHAPTER TEN

Turning the Corner

T HOMASON WAS RELIEVED when the doctor came in and officially released Gabby from the hospital. They provided a three-month supply of meds and a prescription for more if needed for pain. Little did they know, Gabby was leaving for Tuscany and would find another doctor there to continue her care. But, in this case, saying less was more. He didn't want any trials leading to her if someone started asking questions.

He'd called the Uber driver and he was waiting in the pick-up lane at the hospital. He'd just texted him and said, he was waiting, and he texted back, we'll be out in a few minutes–wait. He did.

Gabby was rolled to the curb in the mandatory wheelchair exit from a hospital. The driver popped the trunk and he placed their suitcases in for the ride to the airport. He quickly texted customer service at the airport and said they were on the way. They would meet them at the entrance with a wheelchair and an expedient trip to their airplane for boarding.

He'd made sure he had the TSA approval for bypassing security, so he'd never have to leave her side. She'd come too far, for someone to murder her now.

The car was filled with silence leaving both in their own thoughts. He patted her hand for reassurance as the driver maneuvered through the heavy downtown traffic heading south to the Hartsfield-Jackson Atlanta International Airport.

They arrived at the front entrance and the driver opened Gabby's door and unloaded their baggage. He quickly paid him cash and looked around for the attendant with the wheelchair he'd ordered for her ride through the airport to their international flight.

Within minutes he saw the attendant and together they helped Sydney into the wheelchair being careful of her arms still wrapped in bandages under a light jacket. He breathed a sigh from relief when Gabby was boarded, and they were settled in their first-class seats.

On his salary, he'd never have been able to afford this luxury but putting her safety first, he'd booked his fare with her credit card. The same for his return trip home, for hiding out in first-class had its benefits–no questions asked. He was incognito and intended to stay that way. He was just glad his boss hadn't questioned him about taking all his vacation leave at once.

He glanced over at Gabby and saw her usual olive complexion had turned stark white and her face riddled in pain. He asked the flight attendant for a bottle of water, then quickly went to her backpack and extracted pain meds for the flight. Maybe she'd lie back and sleep through most or all the flight. He could hope.

He passed the hours nodding off occasionally but always knowing where he was and the job at hand–getting Gabby safely inside her villa. Her recovery plans were already established with a new doctor from the region on call in case he was needed.

When the plane landed, she'd be escorted off in a wheelchair, the first to disembark the plane. He was counting down to a peaceful existence at her Tuscany villa. Transportation was arranged with the phone call he made when learning of her release date. A car from her estate would pick them up upon arrival and take them directly to the villa.

She'd told him she had staff there year-round to see to the needs of her visitors. Locals were always ready to work when the villa was occupied. For generations, the families worked in the vineyards or winery year-round. From cooks to housemaids, and a driver, the villa was staffed for an enjoyable stay.

For things to go smoother in the transition, she just had to sell them of her kinship to Sydney, and everything would fall in place. The villa was now in her name Gabrielle D'Agostino and she was sure the staff would treat her with the same respect as on previous visits, even if she was going by an alias now.

The villa was family property and only family, or friends of the family had ever stayed at the villa. They'd gone over her story numerous times. She was confident the attorney handling her final arrangements notified the management of the villa of its new owner when administering the estate.

His identity as Deputy Director of the Georgia Bureau of Investigation, GBI, would never be mentioned. He was a friend accompanying her home and taking a much-needed vacation. Short and simple, the staff had no reason to question his being there.

Gabrielle was groggy when awakened for leaving the plane. The attendant helped her into the wheelchair and off they went to the car parked curbside. The Italian driver was courteous and helped her into the vehicle. He'd popped the trunk prior to their arrival and he quickly stashed their luggage for the drive home.

They rode up and down the winding roads until pulling into the circular driveway and coming to a halt at the double Tuscan mahogany doors with a lion's head knocker prominently displayed at the spacious entryway.

Gabby would need his help to steady her as she walked to her bedroom. Staff members were lined up to greet her and she nodded as she walked by. She knew exactly where her bedroom was and kept a steady pace to her destination ready to lie down after the long flight.

One of the staff members stayed discretely behind them. When Gabby reached her bedroom, she immediately laid down on her bed, not taking the time to change into a nightgown. She was pooped out. He removed her shoes and gently slid her over in the bed tucking the blanket in beside her.

He turned and asked the staff member her name and then to bring water, wine, and fresh fruit to her bedroom. He said he'd like to meet the kitchen staff and go over the menu for tonight and the next few days. Gabrielle would take over from there, he'd said. The staff members were cordial and didn't question his taking over for her and giving them orders. He was relieved. The day had been long already, and he just wanted Gabby to rest and eat a bite, take her meds and sleep.

He was glad her suite was on the bottom level to not push her past her physical limits. While Gabby rested, he looked around the villa and decided on taking the suite next-door to hers, close enough that if she needed him, he'd hear her call.

While roaming through the villa he realized the view from every room was spectacular. He had no idea there was a vineyard and commercial winery on the grounds until today. She'd never mentioned they had their own wine label. But, why should he be surprised? She only talked about what she deemed important at the time. He wondered if he'd ever learned all there was about Sydney Jones. What else was she holding back filed under the heading-need-to-know?

CHAPTER ELEVEN

Stranglehold

GODWIN ITCHED TO avenge Sydney's murder, and he'd discovered the culprit who issued the hit and the sleaze who carried it out. But she was dead so what good would that do except maybe jeopardizing his future of seeing David grow into a man. Every time his thoughts went down that path, he rebuked them and replaced them with happier moments now memories of Sydney and David in their place.

David was smart like his mother and possibly innate with technical skills like himself. He'd been keen on learning more about the technologies industry and with his grades had landed a spot in advanced technologies classes at his high school.

He'd love to adopt him and change his name to Godwin for with his aptitude he'd go to the top in whatever the field he chose. With the last name, Jones, he didn't want him on the CIA's radar, and he was sure he'd make a name for himself in whatever field he pursued.

Being Sydney Jones' son, he'd be marked if the CIA learned of his propensity toward the spy game. He'd try to keep him focused on the business side as he'd already benefited financially from the development of apps they'd worked on together.

David had matured over the last year since his mother's death. Now a junior in high school, Daniela was a stabilizing effect on him, and he listened to her. She'd kept his mother's memories alive by recalling the life they'd lived together. Although Sydney didn't know it, Daniela was the best friend she ever had, and she'd needed one.

Sydney's aunt and only surviving next of kin, Gabrielle, was supposed to relocate to Barbados from Italy according to Daniela. The postcards Daniela had received in David's behalf, said she'd wasn't in the best of health and when she'd planned her trip, she's contracted Shingles, a highly contagious virus, and was unable to leave Tuscany.

Gabrielle must be elderly and susceptible to moray of illnesses. Now, he doubted she'd bring comfort to David regardless of the family relationship. David would be far more active than a spinster was accustomed to being around and especially in charge of raising to adulthood.

Daniela was pregnant with her and Jonathan's first child. He couldn't blame her for wanting to move on with their lives and move into the villa Sydney left them in her will, next door to her dream home, now David's. This all hinged on when Gabrielle, showed up to take over the parenting of David.

In times like these, he wished David's paternity wasn't a secret. He hated to agree, but Sydney was right about not listing him as the father on his birth certificate. The CIA would have used anything, even their son, to make him toe the line. Now, he was paying the price. He checked himself, for the situation could be worst. He was able to spend quality time with his son, and direct him as far as he'd allow.

The days he and David spent sports-fishing were some of their best moments. He'd learned how to navigate the waters into the best fishing around the island. He was proud of him and looked forward to their time on the turquoise Caribbean Ocean.

He'd finally found his match for hauling in the biggest catch of the day. They'd decided to sell their catches to the local restaurants since they docked at the wharf with their coolers and live wells full of the ocean's bounty.

He let David pocket the money from their outings for buying his favorite games and playing his outdoor sports. He always said, thank you. Secretly, he hoped he put some in savings, for although rich from inheritances, who could foretell what he'd want to invest in for the future?

His eyes were on David constantly never knowing if Duane Nelson, his mother's killer, had slipped through the dragnet for him in the states. As a contract killer, he was accustomed to changing his identity and slipping through barriers law enforcement constructed to catch him. He'd keep a check on his employer to see if he'd put out a hit on David. With his vengeance unchecked, and not arrested for Sydney's murder, he might boldly try to end her family line.

ooooo

Duane was tired of the luxury lifestyle at Judith's Puerto Vallarta villa. Just how long can one stare at the Caribbean Sea and interact with the socialites in her residential community? It had all grown old. For a while, after going through Judith's ledger at her villa, he'd found something to occupy his time—taking over Judith's rentals.

The renters had thought they'd gotten off scot-free when they didn't make timely payments. They'd been sliding by since her murder. But that changed when he key-stroked his name in as the owner of the record with her signature stamp. The renters wouldn't be missing any more payments after his personal visit to their homes.

He was bored and needed another adrenaline rush, and following up on Judith's visit to Barbados came to mind. He'd tried once to find leads to her new scheme and failed. The coast looked clear for his return to investigate further. He had a gut feeling he'd missed something important. Damn, he might even follow through on her idea of investing in Barbados, her next real estate island strategy. He booked his flight and packed his bags for leaving the next day.

CHAPTER TWELVE

Mindful Pursuits

SYDNEY WAS SLOWLY mending from the severe burns from the death trap she'd escaped when her Porsche was car bombed. Thomason had long ago returned to Atlanta after his five weeks stay at the villa. She missed him. They stayed in touch by phone and although she had no desire to return to Atlanta, he could meet her on the island or at the villa in Italy or anywhere but where she'd been torched. She'd pay for his travel for he'd been like family before and after her final run-in with criminals' intent on killing her.

She missed David and was ready to relocate to her dream home in Barbados. At every turn, it seemed she had a setback when she was ready to take the next step. Dr. Rossi who Thomason had found in Tuscany to treat her was attentive. She'd even agreed to have more surgery to remove scarring at his medical center with his assurance of minor complications from the procedures.

Her immune system was weakened from the surgeries making her suspectable to many illnesses that in the past wouldn't side-tracked her. She was delayed once again for leaving for Barbados and reuniting with her son, now considered nephew to those who mattered.

Over a year had passed, and she hoped David was maneuvering through his heartbreak and grief. Daniela's response to her postcards had been brief, but thankfully she enclosed photos of David making her smile. He was the spitting image of his father—Walker. She hoped he'd be glad to meet the new family member on her return to the island. She'd missed her only child beyond words.

She gazed into the vintage mirror and gasped in surprise as the redness and discoloration on her face and arms were gone. The rest of her body she could keep covered as they healed from the latest skin grafts. Now, if she could get over the cold she'd come down with, she could book her flight. Her floral tapestry colored bags were packed and ready to go.

Tomorrow would be the day she'd make the smooth transition to the island. The old Italian villa still had its antiquated service call system although it had been renovated in the past 10 years. Craftsmen in the old country liked to tinker and fix systems and appliances eloquently designed and repurposed for reuse.

Using the polished bronze call button, she buzzed her house attendant, Maria, and asked for soup and fruit for lunch. She'd eat and relax in bed, hopefully falling asleep, so her body would regenerate and be ready for her big day. She felt island-bound in every fiber of her body.

○○○○○

Thomason was glad to hear from Gabby and be updated about her continued recovery and plans to reunite with her son, David. He wished he could be present for the reunion but too many questions would be asked if he showed up at the same time.

Perhaps after she settled in, he could make the trip. All he'd have to say is he had time off, and she'd make his flight, in first-class no less, happen. In the meantime, he had investigations to do and thanks to political friends of Sydney Jones her car bombing was still active.

All investigative units were still on full alert. Duane Nelson had slipped through the only sighting they had of him in Montana. He looked like he disappeared in a poof, into thin air, far away from where he was expected to be. The FBI had followed up and found his rustic retreat uninhabited with no personal items and swept clean of prints. He'd vanished, but where?

CHAPTER THIRTEEN

The Homecoming

NELSON'S PLANE TOUCHED down at the Grantley Adams International Airport Barbados airport. He'd booked accommodations at a resort this time hoping to meet a likely bed partner. If there were solo travelers or even girls weekend getaway booked at the same time, he'd help his prospects. He didn't care if they were married if they wanted to hook up for a sexual tryst. He was aroused just thinking about a warm female body.

He could use some women companionship after his stay in Puerto Vallarta in Judith's uppity residential community. What was worse, when he went slumming in bars and likely hookup spots, he'd not connected once with a female. He started hanging out where the cruise ships docked hoping for a pickup. Just about the time, he'd lost hope, a male prostitute became an option. He'd learned to make do to satisfy his sexual urges.

ooooo

Godwin watched on his computer screen as Nelson left the airport. He wondered what his plans were for this trip. He'd soon find out. In the meantime, he needed to keep an eye out for David in case Nelson started sneaking around their home and asking questions.

Having met a real estate agent at the property next door and now knowing the location of Sydney's property could spell danger for David. He had no doubt Nelson realized Sydney was dead. What could he be looking for now? The only answer was he'd learned or suspected a payday from something Judith uncovered on the island before he murdered her. But, obviously, not the whole story, or he'd acted sooner.

Godwin was one step ahead of Nelson by noting his flight's arrival and plans to put a GPS tracker on the car rental reserved in his name. He'd know every step he made and keep David occupied doing the activities he enjoyed.

He wished Nelson would crawl back into the pitch-black dung hole, he came from and never return to their paradise. His mind slid into the warrior mode thinking of the possibilities if Nelson had booked a fishing trip on one of his charters. Then, again, that would have been too easy, he thought. And, life had never been easy for him.

ooooo

Gabrielle leaves for the island...

Gabrielle was wheeled into the Galileo Galilei International Airport in Pisa Italy with her driver accompanying her as far as security would allow him. She thanked him and said, she'd see them again once she was settled.

She felt healthy enough to walk but her staff had become like family and insisted she save her energy for the long flight. She took their suggestion and was pleased with the early seating aboard the aircraft. Now, she could sit back and read until she could see her son, David, again.

She'd have time to think about their meeting on the flight. As much as she'd like to wrap her arms around him and smell his scent, she had to remember he'd never truly met the aunt. She would have to reign in her emotions and jubilance for seeing him again and act the part of his only next-of-kin aunt who'd not seen him since he was a baby. A difficult task at best.

ooooo

Godwin was having his morning coffee when David came by before school on his motorcycle. He wondered what news he had that couldn't wait until the afternoon.

He watched as he secured his bike slamming his kickstand in place on a level spot in the driveway. He opened the screen door smiling, and said, "Good morning!"

"Good morning, yourself. What brings you by early this morning?"

"I thought you should know my aunt, Gabrielle, is arriving tomorrow."

"You don't say? Weren't you expecting her?"

"Yes, but I don't know how to act when I meet her?"

"Just treat her with respect and help her when she needs it. From what you've said, she's frail and could probably use a helping hand."

A frown creased David's face. "What am I to do now? Daniela plans to move next door after she gets settled in, so they can make plans and get the house organized for their new baby. And, I'll be alone with an elderly lady."

"It can't be all that bad for after all she's kinfolks, the only one you have left."

"You can say that for you don't live there."

"Right, and I'll be here when you need a sounding board."

"Yeah, I knew I could count on you. One more thing, will you drive me to the airport to pick her up?" A tight smile crept across his lips.

"I think I can handle that. Call me with the time she's supposed to arrive, and I'll pick you up to welcome her to our island."

"Thanks!"

"Your welcome. Now off to school with yourself. I'll see you afterward, and we'll dangle our hooks in the ocean for a fresh catch for Gabrielle's arrival."

David waved goodbye before lifting his helmet hanging from the handlebars and readying himself before riding off toward his school.

Godwin completed the technologies work for his clients around the globe and sat back noting it was almost time for David to arrive after school. He quickly called Daniela to remind her he was coming by, just in case he forgot to tell her when leaving for his early morning mission. He asked about grilling fresh fish for dinner and his driving David to the airport for her arrival.

Daniela was glad for his help with David and thankful for his taking charge of Gabrielle's homecoming to their villa. He could tell her pregnancy was draining her energy and hoped when Gabrielle arrived, she'd provide some relief.

He and David had another fishing expedition that'd make even the most accomplished fisherman's day. They sold some of their catch at the wharf and he wrapped others to take home to prepare for Gabrielle's first dinner on the island.

ooooo

Godwin was up early and quickly phoned David to see if he was dressed and ready to meet Gabrielle at the airport. When David answered his lackluster tone was a dead giveaway. He wasn't looking forward to the changes thrust upon him.

This was a pivotal point for David, and he wanted to see him safely through it. He'd just have to quicken his pace and help David come to terms with the next stage in his life. He drove over to pick him up wondering how the meeting would go.

They rode in silence each in their own thoughts about the new permanent house guest. He parked near the entrance to the Grantley Adams International Airport and waited for David's aunt to appear. Not having a picture of her, but with the timing being right-on, he figured the lady in the wheelchair with the Italian luggage beside her was most likely David's next of kin.

He quickly spoke to David who immediately got out of the car to greet her. Godwin took her luggage and stuffed it into his oversized trunk, remembering past feats of different cargo when Sydney was alive.

David helped her into the backseat of the luxury automobile, and he quickly introduced himself as Jim Godwin, a friend of David's and the family. She said, "Hello, and thanks for picking me up from the airport. I've looked forward to this for a long time."

Looking in his rearview mirror he could see the flight of nearly seventeen hours had taken a toll on her body. She'd need to rest when arriving at the oceanfront villa. He could see the smile on David's face probably a relief for she wasn't the elderly person he'd expected. In fact, she was quite beautiful in a lovely Italian way.

On arrival, David opened the car door, and she asked him to hold out his arm to steady her as she walked into the villa. Tears filled her eyes on entering the magnificent architecturally designed home, and he wondered if she was thinking about Sydney.

Daniela met them at the front entry with a smile on her face. He had no idea what was going on in her mind, but she started bawling maybe it was from her emotional state from her pregnancy. But he found himself comforting two women and had no idea why both were having a meltdown.

He waited for it to pass and Daniela went into the kitchen and brought back a small glass of wine for Gabrielle and a crystal glass filled with sparkling water for herself, and toasted her arrival. He didn't expect this welcoming tribute but was glad the two were friends, nonetheless. This would make David's transition easier through the days and months ahead.

Daniela asked if he'd show Gabrielle to her suite, and make her comfortable after her long flight. He responded in the affirmative glad to be of service and the crying ended. David followed wanting to be of help and learn more about Gabrielle.

Her bedroom suite was upstairs, and he was glad Sydney had workman install an elevator for quick access to the upper level for he doubted in her emotional state and fatigue she could climb the stairs. He and David rode the elevator with her and placed her luggage in Sydney's old bedroom suite. He told her to rest after her flight and he'd bring up some soup and crackers, and fruit to refuel her energy. She thanked him and said, "I can't wait to change into something more tropical and relaxing."

"Sure, I'll be back in a few minutes with your lunch."

David followed him out the door with a questioning look on his face. He'd talk to him later about the concern that flashed across his face. He realized this was a heavy burden for a teen to carry. Gabrielle would need some help until she was fully recovered. He'd met a nice creole lady who'd be the perfect fit for making this transition easier for all. It was the least he could do under the circumstances and didn't mind footing the costs if Daniela agreed for now.

He liked the sound of Gabrielle's voice. Although speaking English her Italian accent was prominent and spunky bringing a flashback of Sydney to mind. He'd like to learn more about her and what caused her physical condition, hopefully not something hereditary for David's sake.

After bringing her lunch into her bedroom suite, he said goodbye until later when he would cook everyone's dinner on the terrace. She smiled and said, "I look forward to seeing you again."

"You can bet on that for with Daniela's pregnancy I plan to pitch in around here."

That evening when he arrived David and Gabrielle were on the terrace talking. He didn't want to interrupt, so he went into the kitchen to prepare the Wahoo and sides for grilling. Daniela wobbled in and thanked him for cooking dinner. Jonathan would come over in a few minutes from his office next door in their new home. He was working long hours trying to get ahead and be ready when the baby arrived to help her take care of the baby. He suggested they hire a nanny, so they both could get some rest. He was sure an islander would be glad to help with their new baby until she was steady on her feet.

ooooo

He went to light the grill on the terrace for cooking their dinner and had already brought out the silverware and plates they'd need and placed them on the oblong table overlooking the Caribbean. Tonight, he was cooking family-style rather than plating each individually. He would place the entrée and sides where the diners could choose their favorites.

The ceiling fans rotated noiseless, breathing soft swirls of air down upon them. Jonathan arrived and after giving Daniela a honey-I'm home kiss, he came out on the terrace to meet David's aunt and to welcome her to the island.

From the startled look in his eyes, he'd guess he was thinking along the lines of David and himself, expecting an elderly lady. He was pleased when he smiled and told her how much they'd looked forward to her arrival.

The seafood dinner was enjoyed by all and although Gabrielle wanted to help clear the table, he said, stay and enjoy the conversation with David, Daniela, and Jonathan. She smiled and said, "Thank you, and please call me Gabby."

He returned a short time later and could see the fatigue in Gabby's face. He asked, "Are you ready to call it a night? I'll be glad to escort you to your suite."

"Yes, thank you. The conversation has been wonderful, and I hope we can continue this tomorrow."

David was out of his chair pulling back hers in a flash and crooked his arm for her to grasp as they returned to her suite. Right now, he couldn't be prouder of his son.

Seeing David would escort Gabby to her suite, he said goodnight to everyone. He'd be phoning his creole friend tomorrow morning about nursing her. Without a doubt, David would be at his front door tomorrow morning wanting to talk about Gabrielle.

They had the weekend for discussion and making plans. He and David would shop for dinner tomorrow from the local farmer's market to change up the seafood cuisine. He loved to cook, and Sydney had brought that out in him. This was the perfect time to repay her for allowing him to grow his skills on her watch.

CHAPTER FOURTEEN

The Guardian

GODWIN OPENED HIS eyes and saw the sun rising over the Caribbean. He got up and put his coffee pot on the stove. He loved his coffee perked and although a technologies wiz, he enjoyed the old-fashioned way for brewing his morning coffee. David would arrive shortly with lots of questions that he had no answers for. However, he could make life flow into a routine by calling his friend and planning for Gabby's care.

Gabby, as she asked to be called, was far from being elderly and whatever caused her diminished capacity, he had no idea but wanted to believe this was a short-lived incapacity. She was too beautiful to be crippled and unable to enjoy life. He could tell from their brief encounter she had spunk. For David and her sake, he hoped she was a prizefighter and would win the battle to be whole again.

ooooo

He was watching every move Nelson made on the island. He was held up at the resort he'd booked for lodging. Maybe he'd stay there the entire time for a vacation. He had too much to do to be shadowing him with the Joneses Caribbean domicile going through an adjustment period. One that he had no choice but to be a part of for David's sake.

He drank his beloved fresh morning brew with coffee beans from Wyndham's, a local coffee roaster. He'd just finished a cup when David rang the door chime politely, for he had a key and could enter anytime. He saw him through the oversized window and got up to unlock the door.

He waved him in and could tell he'd had a sleepless night. He told him his favorite soft drink was in the frig to help himself. He did. Then sat at the breakfast table in a daze. Godwin asked, "What's wrong?"

He said, "I've been having a Deja vu feeling since Gabrielle arrived. It's like we're connected but I don't know-how. I don't remember meeting her as a baby before Daniela started taking care of me."

"Well, David, she is family. And, she may remind you of your mother although they don't look the same. You may have a spiritual connection because of familial backgrounds."

"I wonder what's wrong with her. Why she can't walk without it being painful? She's young after all so maybe she'll get better."

"David, most likely she'll improve, or she'd not left Italy and her doctors to come here."

"I hope that's the case, for she seems like a real nice lady and one I'd like to become friends with."

"David, I've found a caregiver for your aunt until she's healthier. I've already talked to Daniela and said this is my gift to the family and I'll continue cooking the evening meals because I enjoy doing it."

"Thank you! I'm sure Daniela and Jonathan want to move over to their home before the baby is born. Maybe this will inspire them to take the next step."

"We've got this—you and I together will make the best of this situation." They bumped knuckles like teammates celebrating a win.

Godwin said, "Come on let's go pick up your new caregiver and tell Daniela and Jonathan they can move out when they're ready. Lulu will stay on the premises and provide the care needed. She's also an accomplished creole cook, for making you and your meals when I'm not around."

David smiled for the first time since entering the front door.

CHAPTER FIFTEEN

Untamed

NELSON WAS HAVING the time of his life on the island. Finally, women were interested in him. The reluctant hoity-toity bitches from Puerto Vallarta were a distant memory from the past. He was with a different woman every night. His sexual cravings were being satisfied just the way he liked them, rough and tough and these women liked it. Little did they know he could've inflicted some real pain into their sexual deviation. But he held himself back remembering the reason he narrowly escaped capture in Montana.

Now he was focused on business to discover the payday Judith was expecting from what she learned here. Damn, he wished he hadn't slit her throat until after she talked. And, she would've.

He decided to look around Sydney Joneses villa. Although she was dead, there still may be something he overlooked in his previous trip to the island. He drove his rental car slowly by her villa and noticed a teenager parking his bike in the garage. He went to the dead-end of the coastal road and turned around hoping to get a better look.

The drive-through on his return pass by the villa sent up fireworks in his mind. The teenager was Dan Walker's kid for he was a spitting image for not many males are over 6' 5" tall as a teenager. That was what Judith planned to blackmail Sydney with. But she was dead now, so how could he benefit? Who could he blackmail? Walker and Sydney both were dead.

Damn, Nelson thought. I killed Judith too soon. I should have questioned her more knowing she was always scheming before slitting her throat. She was onto a big payday with Sydney Jones. This time he did himself in for Sydney wasn't around to blackmail, but her son—well he'd see what angle he could use. Perhaps, the U.S. government would like to be informed that Dan Walker has a son.

ooooo

Godwin felt it in every fiber of his being, danger, was ahead. He hated his native premonitions although they'd warned him of what lies ahead.

The sinking feeling of doom and gloom comes over him and he must fight his way out. Sometimes the darkness stays until the ordeal is over and then he sees sunlight once again. He wonders if this will be the case this time. What did he miss?

He goes to his computer where he's in effect watching the world around him and starts streaming video of the Joneses residence on the island, where his son lives. Knowing his love for David is the closest thing that could signal this distress, he decides to take a closer look.

There on his screen, he sees Nelson casing the Joneses home. And, to make matters worse David was in clear view in the driveway parking his motorcycle. But what could Nelson be after? Both he and Sydney were dead leaving no one for him to blackmail–unless he was planning to scheme David about his father being a burned spy before his death, making him look unpatriotic at best and putting him on the CIA's radar.

He hoped he was just on a fact-finding mission knowing some of what Judith was up to before he murdered her and realize it was too late to blackmail Sydney or himself. Well, David, he doubted would give him the time of day, but he'd be vigilant in making sure Nelson didn't get anywhere with his newfound knowledge.

CHAPTER SIXTEEN

At the Crossroads

GABBY WALKED OUT on the balcony overlooking the downstairs living area with a backdrop of a sunlit Caribbean ocean shining through the oversized windows. She marveled at how far she'd come since returning to her dream home in Barbados.

Lulu the creole woman taking care of her was making the household run smoothly. Having known Daniela all her life she'd convinced her to make the move next door to their new home and begin planning for their baby's arrival.

Lulu moved into a downstairs bedroom suite and was comfortable being the watchdog for her new family. She made teas using special Bajan recipes, and poultices from local herbs for her reddened and blotched skin hidden beneath her clothes. Lulu wanted her to be healthy again and she took special care of David always wanting him to share his plans for the day.

David was always towering over her when cooking wanting to learn the special Bajan ingredients she used in her recipes. He had a knack for making Bajan dishes already from Daniela and Godwin who had taken over making the evening meals. Lulu mentioned she liked the feel of their home—loving. Adding she believed it was her presence that made it so. The home was blessed, it radiated in every fiber of her being.

If she only knew the nightmarish hell the family had experienced, Gabby thought. Nonetheless, she was glad Lulu had made a home with them and was helping the family to become whole again.

Godwin showed up just in time to get the evening meal ready for the family. He'd stopped by the local market and bought chicken and fresh vegetables to make his baked Bajan Chicken dish.

Gabby went downstairs to the kitchen and sat on a bar stool as Godwin prepared dinner. He moved with the fluid grace of a tiger back and forth between the stove and prep area. The kitchen was filled with a delightful aroma with the herbs and spices creating a flavorful and mouth-watering scent.

David came in sweaty with his t-shirt soaked and said hello on the way to his bedroom suite to shower and change. He'd been playing basketball with his friends from school. He commented in passing that a man he'd never seen before was watching their game from a parked car. "Kind of spooky, if you ask me," he said.

"Did you get a good look at him?" Walker asked with a frown creasing his once smiling face.

"Yes, but I've not seen him before." He went on to describe the man he'd seen in the black sedan parked across from the basketball court.

Godwin took a deep breath and exhaled. "Next time you see him, snap a photo and send it to me."

"Will do," he said. "Just wondered what he was up to?"

"I'll look into it. In the meantime, you guys need to stick together and not go off alone."

"Don't worry," he said. We look out for one another knowing we play in a touristy area."

"Good," said Godwin. "Stay safe."

Godwin had a sneaking suspension the stalker was Nelson. But what was he up to?

Already, Godwin recognized David had a keen sense of danger, one that spies live and die by. This was a good thing if he didn't become one. For he knew that road well, for the life he wanted with Sydney had been destroyed because of his being targeted for company business.

ooooo

Nelson is convinced the young man he followed to the basketball court is the son of the burned spy, Dan Walker. This must have been the payday Judith was aiming for but who was the blackmail target, surely not the son. She'd go directly to the money holder.

She'd uncovered something more and he intended to find out what. Staying a little longer in Barbados wouldn't be a bad gig since he couldn't return to Montana and didn't like Judith's expat community. Besides, he was meeting women at the resort where he was staying, another bonus.

He planned to keep an eye on the young man and follow him about hoping he'd lead him to the verifiable proof he needed to carry out Judith's blackmail scheme. In the least, he'd find out who held the purse strings for his blackmail plan.

Knowing the ends and outs of tailing without becoming suspect, he returned his car to the airport rentals and exchanged for another. This way he could keep his identity shielded a little longer while he collected information. Then he'd strike hard with absolute power to gain his payday.

ooooo

Godwin was at his computer early tracking Nelson's movements. When he saw him return to the rental agency and park the car, he realized his cagey move had a purpose. Now, he couldn't monitor his movement and find out what he was up to.

David would make his customary stop on his way to school. Without frightening him, he wanted him to pay close attention to his surroundings and report back if he was being followed.

His son had been through enough with the death of his mother, he didn't need any added drama in his life. His palms became sweaty just thinking about him being in harm's way.

He leaned back in his desk chair and thought about David. Sydney had enrolled him in martial arts when he was in elementary school. Being a martial artist herself and a physically strong woman, she wanted him to learn the ropes to defend himself. He continued to learn and compete up until Sydney was murdered and he moved to the island with Daniela.

He was a natural at Judo with his strong body and long legs. A leg sweep against an opponent would give him the upper hand in combat. He wondered how much training he remembered and if he practiced.

Living on the island he wouldn't have the sparring partners as he did at his Atlanta dojo. He'd feel better knowing David was in top form for this could just be the beginning. Only time would tell the scum bags waiting to cash in with details about him and his life as a burned CIA agent or from Sydney's sworn enemies.

He remembered the mats he had stored in his basement and decided to ask David for a match to look over his form and skills. If he enjoyed it, he could ask his best friend over and they could practice in secret. Being able to protect himself was important, and the focus learned from practicing martial arts would tune his perception and boost his confidence. He hoped he'd not slacked off by at least practicing Tai Chi, a slow-motion martial art until needed in battle.

ooooo

David stopped by Godwin's on the way home from school and had his usual herbal shake. "Do you want to go fishing?" asked David.

"Perhaps, later. What about we do some martial arts training? I bet you've not been on a mat since leaving Atlanta."

"What's going on? First you warn me about strangers, now you want me to spar with you."

"I just want you to be in top form to protect yourself."

"Oh, I see. And, this came to you suddenly?"

"Well, you're growing up and I didn't want you to fall out of practice."

A smug look came across David's face. "Ok, old man, let's see what you got. I figure you've got some mats around here someplace. Let's go-at-it."

"You're right about that. Follow me. There are mats in the basement already thrown down for our match."

"Then can we go fishing?"

"Yep, we'll catch dinner and sell some at the dock if we're lucky."

CHAPTER SEVENTEEN

Sounding the Alarm

GABBY WAS ON the terrace overlooking the Caribbean ocean with the sunlight dancing off the waves. She believed this was her refuge. She'd wished a thousand times, at least, since being blown up in her car, she'd never returned to Atlanta. She'd been safe on the island and her son wouldn't be calling her auntie.

She was talking on her cell with Thomason. He was updating her about the manhunt for Duane Nelson. His investigators had tracked him to Judith Garner's Puerto Vallarta holdings under an alias. He'd since left there according to the HOA office at Judith's community and headed to Barbados. He wanted her to be vigilant in protecting herself and son. He wasn't sure what he'd discovered, but he was on to something pertaining to her, and he had his suspicions.

Gabby said, "I can't protect myself from a flea, let alone protect my son. I thought this was over."

"Sydney is dead as far as the world knows. He won't be coming for Sydney Jones for he thinks he'd killed you. I'm worried about David."

"He's a teenager and is finally enjoying his high school life. I don't know how to talk to him about this."

"Gabby listen to me. Call Godwin and tell him you're concerned for yours and David's safety and ask him to move into one of your downstairs bedrooms until we find out what Nelson is up to. He's over there all the time, didn't you say, making dinner. He'll jump at the chance to be close to you and your son."

"You make it sound so easy. But, with my son's life in danger, I'll ask him."

"Do that, and get back with me."

The hits keep coming, she thought. Like this good-looking man about town is going to change his life at her biding. She wished she was stronger, but desiring it wouldn't make her stand on her own two feet any faster. She had no other choice but to do what Thomason suggested.

ooooo

In a neighboring community, Godwin gets to witness and review David's martial arts capabilities. Well, he called himself sneaking a preview, but David's uncanny reasoning skills called his bluff. They had started a match on an earlier visit, but David refused to get serious and they called it quits for the day and went fishing.

His new German Shepherd, Harley, welcomed him as far as his breed goes, by allowing him into his home. David threw him a treat from his satchel, and he was reminded Harley was to be a gift to the family after training. And, David's respect and growing fondness for her would go a long way when making the transition to her new home.

He was always prepared with a treat, and he couldn't wait until he learned Harley was his. He'd be surprised and thrilled with the gift of a growing bundle of fur.

"Are you ready to show me your takedowns?" asked Godwin.

"No time like the present, for me to teach you a thing or two." David laughed.

Following one after the other downstairs to the basement and his workout room, he realized today's match would be a tell-all. They warmed up with stretches before beginning their match. Godwin was right, David went for the leg sweep first and it was a powerful move. The ashi-waza techniques are not easy to master but when performed right these are some of the most magnificent throws in the world of Judo.

He'd expected his first move, but his enemies wouldn't. He countered with a harai goshi putting a surprised look on David's face followed by David's perfect execution of an uchi mata sukashi.

Taking a needed break, he asked David if he'd been taught the choke moves. He said no. He proceeded to show him the most dangerous and fatal moves you can make on an enemy–taking their last breath.

They continued their workout allowing David some practice chokes on himself before tapping out. Sweating and breathless, he finished the match and learned martial arts came second nature to David. He'd remembered all the basic moves and showed top form in grappling.

"So, how have you been staying in shape on the island? There's no dojo here."

"I practice Tai Chi beside the pool overlooking the Caribbean before heading over here and then to school. I do it more on the island than I did in our home gym back in Atlanta. But, thanks to our mirrored gym, I was able to perfect my stance and become fluid in movement. The practice relaxes and helps me focus."

He said, "David if you want to ask your best friend over and teach him here, I'm fine with that. Being prepared is a good thing especially living on a tourist island where there are lots of strangers. Who knows someone may try to pickpocket you one day?"

"Let'em try."

"My point exactly."

"Enough said, now can we go fishing?"

"Yep, the *Eclipse* is fueled and ready for our fishing trip."

"I'd hoped to not be disappointed." He laughed.

The fishing trip was bountiful. They docked and Godwin sent texts to the restaurant chefs he sold to and told them he had fresh fish. He sold most of their catch, setting aside dinner for him and David's household. He was looking forward to seeing the lovely Gabby and an evening with his son.

David rode his motorcycle home ahead of Godwin who's stayed behind to shower after their fishing trip. Just before he leaned in to push his bike into the garage at home, he saw a new sedan driving by slowly with a man behind the steering wheel. He wondered if that was the same man, he saw at the basketball court. But the car was a different model, and it didn't make sense for someone to be following him home.

Still, he promised Godwin he'd call him if he saw anything strange. He did.

"I thought you'd want to know; a strange car appeared to follow me home after leaving the docks."

"Go inside, I'll be there in a minute. And, don't answer the door unless it's me!"

Godwin shook his head, thinking it was likely Nelson tracking David's movements. Sooner or later, he'd probably confront him to get answers to his questions. He'd verify the make and model of the car to see if it was the same one from the rental agency he traded for after David saw him earlier.

He had no idea how to protect David and possibly Gabby. He'd been riding his bike to their home lately to park it in the garage out of sight. David always made sure he was parked leaving ample space in their oversized garage.

David went into the house and said hello to Lulu and washed his hands in the kitchen sink. He'd loved to take a shower but decided with the alarm in Godwin's voice, he needed to stay near the front door in case Lulu heard the doorbell and answered it.

He never doubted there were secrets about his mother's death he hadn't learned. He had his suspicions, but they were unverified since Daniela couldn't talk about his mother without getting upset. And, being pregnant now, it was out of the question. But Godwin knew something, and he'd find out what. Now, was as good a time as ever.

He was sitting in the downstairs living area when Godwin arrived and came through the garage door. Normally, he went around to the front entrance and rang the doorbell. He had their fresh catch with him cleaned and ready to cook.

Grilled fish sounded good and Gabby would enjoy the exotic flavorings he used and the aroma of the fresh spices and herbs. Then, after dinner, he'd question him about his stalker.

ooooo

Gabby rode the elevator downstairs and met them on the terrace. She appeared like a fresh breath of air and greeted everyone. She wanted to hug David and decided not to. Godwin was as good-looking as he was the last time he was there. She had to catch herself and remember to stay clear of involvement. He reminded her of Walker, probably from his size and height. And, she didn't want to think about him for it was depressing.

She'd decided to talk with him after dinner about what Thomason had said. Since she was supposing next of kin to Sydney, his calling her with an update about Sydney's murder wouldn't be suspicious. Yet, her son and Daniela were told it was a car accident and left Atlanta for Barbados before the news hit the headlines.

She freshens her drink and sets the table for dining on the terrace. Lulu would be joining them shortly for she enjoyed Godwin's grilling rather than cooking their homestyle dinner. The conversation was light, but she noticed David whispering something to Godwin. She wondered what that was about? Hopefully their next fishing trip.

She found herself counting down the minutes until she could talk with Godwin in private. She was unsure if David could handle the truth about his mother's murder. He'd already had a tough time grieving and didn't need an added burden of learning her death was not an accident as originally stated.

∞∞∞

Lulu began clearing the table and setting fresh flowers where the fish platter once was. Since dinner was over, she hoped David would go upstairs to shower for he still wore the same clothes from his fishing trip. Then she could talk with Godwin without fear of his overhearing. David helped Lulu take the dishes to the kitchen. This was her chance to tell Godwin she needed to talk with him privately.

"Godwin," she said. "I'd like to have a word with you before you go home."

"Sure," he said. Although, puzzled by her request for she'd been distant since her arrival. She usually left for her suite early after dinner. Now, he had both David and her to talk with tonight. Secrets. What's next?

∞∞∞

Gabby decided David must have gone upstairs to shower and decided to talk with Godwin in his absence. She said, "Thomason from the Atlanta GBI called me today." She waited for his response noting the scowl across his face.

"And, what did he have to report?" he asked.

He said, "They'd tracked Nelson from his hideout in Montana to Puerto Vallarta where he'd taken over Judith's properties using an alias. Now, he's in Barbados and he's concerned about our safety. He suggested I ask you to move in downstairs until he's off the island or captured."

105

The look on Gabby's face was priceless, he thought. She didn't want to ask him for help but needed to.

"That's not a problem," he said. "So, what have you learned about Sydney's death?"

"It was no accident as initially reported."

"I see. And, you're aware that Nelson is the murderer?"

"Yes!"

"Well, that makes two of us."

"Does David know?"

"No, I think he suspects foul play but was told it was an accident before it was investigated further."

"He's a smart kid and will figure it out whether we tell him or not."

"The police are tracking Nelson, perhaps we should wait."

"He's on the Internet. When he's arrested, he'll see it and wonder why we didn't tell him sooner."

"You've got a point. Perhaps, we should talk to him together? I'll let you do the talking since I'm his distant aunt."

She hated lying, but to keep her own identity secret she had no choice.

"Do you feel up to talking with him tonight?"

"Yes, I rested some during the day and feel fine."

They left the terrace reluctantly for the view of the sunset was awe-inspiring. They were seated on the sofa when David returned squeaky clean with wet hair after his shower.

David looked from one to the other and said, "What's up?"

"We need to talk to you," said Godwin. In the back of his mind, he wondered if he should tell him his father was a burned spy for that could be Nelson's lead in conversation starter. He'd take his time and see how David accepted the news they were going to disclose.

"Your aunt had a call from the GBI about your mother's accident."

"So, do I get the full story now?"

"Yes," said Gabby.

Godwin continued with the report of Nelson as the murderer of his mother and on the run from law enforcement now in Barbados.

"So, do you think the man following me is him?"

"Could be. I'll cross-reference the automobile you saw today with his airport rental."

"Someone's been following you?" asked Gabby.

"Yes, since the weekend."

"Next time, tell me, please."

"Ok, if that'll make you feel better."

"I do now."

Gabby said, "Thomason suggested Godwin stay with us until Nelson was off the island or arrested."

"It's a done deal," said Godwin. "I'll go back home tomorrow and get more clothes, personal items, and Harley. Tonight, I'm staying and remember no one is to answer the door, but me."

"Loud and clear! Are you really bringing the little scout?" said David.

"Yes, he's yours if Gabby doesn't mind. I was training him as a gift for you."

David glanced in Gabby's direction and she nodded her approval.

"Thank you. Harley likes me and I'm sure you can train her here now."

"Yes, and you can help with the training and her care. We'll consider her yours starting tomorrow. One other thing, if Nelson should approach you, he may begin the conversation by asking you about your father and question you about his being a burned spy. Apparently, he's put together your background and would want to use it as a bargaining tool with the CIA when captured. He'll try blackmail on his initial contact for that's been his go-to strategy in the past.

"My father died when I was young and there was no mention of him being a spy. Mother just said, he was head of her security for the office and home. And, they developed a special relationship."

"Well, he was a CIA operative although it was not his choice at the time. So, don't let Nelson rattle you if you're approached by him."

"Not to worry about me, it's him you need to concern yourself with for paybacks can be hell."

"By the way, If the local police know he's on the island why don't they arrest him?"

"I wish it were that simple. The United States and Barbados do have a mutual extradition treaty, but it takes time and manpower to put it in place. Plus, he's a slick one making him difficult to capture."

Looking over at Gabby, he asked, "Can't Thomason speed things up a bit?"

"I'm sure he's working on it," said Gabby. "In the meantime, watch your back."

"Don't worry, I will."

After the heavy conversation, each said good-night and went to their bedrooms. Godwin tucked the pistol he always carried under his pillow before lying down to sleep. Perhaps, it was time to buy David his own gun. They'd been practicing at his range and he was an accurate shooter. Extra protection might come in handy for as the saying goes, 'you never carry a knife to a gunfight'.

CHAPTER EIGHTEEN

Just Cause

NELSON WAS MAPPING out his strategy for putting a hit on David to collect the remainder of the monies on his contract to kill. Finding him wasn't a crapshoot, for he'd trailed him for several days and found his routine seldom varied. He was just a schoolboy who spent a lot of time with his friends and the charter boat captain at the wharf then returned home by sundown. Killing him would be easy if he was away from the Bridgetown docks.

He wanted to do the hit where the body would be easily disposed of and catch the next flight to Belize. He liked these English-speaking islands and with the right opportunity, he'd settle somewhere along the coast. But not where he did hits for that would complicate shielding his identity.

Finally, he decided to attack David on his way home riding his motorcycle. He planned to drive up beside him and open fire. With luck, he and his motorcycle would go over the cliff at the place he designated, a dangerous curve easily an accident site. He took a deep draw from his Cuban cigar, and thought-the Jones family is accident-prone. He smiled at the thought.

Gabby was on the phone with Thomason listening to his recent activity to bring Nelson to justice. The problem was Nelson had changed aliases again since leaving Mexico and they'd not been able to pinpoint the name he was using in Barbados. She noted the exasperation in his voice when delivering the news and wanted assurance Godwin was living at her home for protection.

She said yes, he'd moved in and thanked him for staying in touch and doing everything possible to capture Nelson. After the call, she lay back on her pillow and thought about her son hoping he was safe.

ooooo

David was leaving school and looked around as he readied himself for his ride to the docks were Godwin said at break-fast, he'd meet him after school. Godwin had scared Lulu half to death by telling her to not open the door unless the caller was known. He really didn't want to fish today although he loved it. He was concerned for Gabby and Lulu at home. He hoped Godwin just needed some help cleaning the boat for the next charter. They'd be done in no time working together.

He rode up to the wharf and parked his bike looking around as he fiddled with making sure his motorcycle was stable. He'd taken Godwin's message to heart and was vigilant in surveying his surroundings.

He walked over to the *Eclipse* and noted it was sparkling clean. He hated to disappoint Godwin, but it wasn't up to a fishing trip. Godwin said, "Climb aboard I've got something to show you."

"Sure," he said, as he stepped over into the 45ft Nor-tech fishing yacht, a supercharged 452 *Superfish* luxury vessel with four tuna tubes by your rods, two 60-gallon live wells and air-conditioning below deck.

Godwin waved him below deck and said, "I trust I can give this to you for your protection and Gabby will never discover our secret."

David's interest was piqued. "So, that's why you wanted to meet here and not at home?"

"You catch on quick. I wanted to make sure you can load and fire this pistol and thought we'd go to a safe place for you to become accustomed to handling this weapon."

David hurriedly released the tie lines and in minutes they were skimming across the water to Godwin pigeonhole, far enough from the coastline to where bullet shots wouldn't be heard. Godwin idled the boat and came about before killing the motors. Then he said, "Let me see you load and fire," as he got ready to toss a mango into the air.

David was quick and fired off his shot directly into the mango he'd tossed. He had dozens onboard and kept tossing with varying angles to keep David off guard. When the crate was empty, he said, "I believe you can handle your weapon. I got you a holster to camouflage it when carrying. Keep it on your bike when at school locked in your leather motorcycle saddlebag. Unlock it when leaving and have it on your body."

"Yes, sir," he said. "Does that mean I'm recruited in the military now." He laughed.

"David, this is no laughing matter your life may be in jeopardy and I'm not always with you. You need to be able to protect yourself."

"I understand. I was just trying to lighten things up."

"Good, we agree."

Godwin hated things had gotten morbid, but he's been on the dark web and verified Ming's son had issued a hit on David and a willing mercenary had taken the contract. He figured Nelson was the hitman and here. Making matters worse and believing Nelson would fail there'd be more after him until Chang Bohai was stopped. He'd already had Sydney killed and wanted to end the family line-his family.

Godwin docked the boat and David helped with the tie downs and said, "I'll see you at home. As he disembarked, he yelled back, I think Lulu is cooking tonight so don't worry about dinner."

He noticed David had his gun holstered and waved as he saddled his motorcycle for the ride home. He double-checked his boat's tie-downs before stepping ashore. He'd meet David at his home.

Only a few minutes ahead of him, he drove in silence and concentrated on the road. He came upon a dark sedan and wondered if he'd pass David on his motorcycle. Up ahead there was a space for traffic to pass before going into the Deadman's curve. The sedan didn't take the fast lane, rather it slowed to stay behind David's motorcycle. His attention peaked for likely Nelson was the driver in front of him following David.

The driver of the black sedan came up beside David's motorcycle and started firing. He pressed hard on the gas pedal and was on his bumper but couldn't hit him without throwing David and his motorcycle off the edge of the cliff.

Suddenly, David maneuvered his bike in an abrupt turnabout facing the sedan and fired directly at the driver in the sedan. In quick motion, he repeated until the sedan went over the cliff at Deadman's curve.

Godwin stopped his car in the middle of the road for there was no place to pull off. David was on his bike facing him and with a thumbs up he turned his bike towards home and kicked it. Godwin followed thinking that's our son-bad to the bone.

ooooo

David and Walker were glued to the TV news channel hoping to hear about the fatal accident on Deadman's curve. Harley was on the couch between them looking from one to the other for attention. When she was petted, she rolled over and went to sleep.

Lulu cooked a delicious Bajan dinner spiced just right for their palate. Gabby came down from her suite for dinner and asked, "How was your day?"

Just so-so was the mumbled mutual reply. She fiddled with the lamp switch aware they were lying. There was something the two of them were hiding. But, what?

They didn't have to wait long before the news channel announced a driver failed to negotiate Deadman's curve and went over the ravine into the ocean. The police were investigating the accident with further reports later.

Gabby didn't need them to tell her about their day. The news explained it all. But who or were both involved?

Hopefully, they'd explain for if weapons were involved perhaps Thomason would help. In times like these, she wished there were no secrets between them. At least Godwin would understand her desire to be involved. She was David's mother. How was she to carry this off as his distant aunt?

Gabby sensed her son was in danger. But now, Godwin and David were hiding secrets and being the distant aunt from Italy she wasn't in the loop. She thought she'd shared enough they'd recognize she was aware of Sydney's background. Perhaps they thought she was too fragile to be told the truth?

She was stronger now than when she arrived. But perhaps their first impressions left them thinking she was an invalid. God, she wished she was stronger, and her legs would hold her up for lengthy periods of time. All she did was rest-but for what?

She'd hoped to develop a relationship with David, but he seemed past the point of caring about his aunt who failed to show after his mother's death.

She hurried outside to the terrace for she felt like screaming. Her life was insane tripped up by secrets she couldn't disclose. Slowly she regained her composure for the two guys inside were apt at uncovering lies. She'd return when the fury subsided.

While she was away, Godwin said, "We need to ditch the gun in case the police want to investigate although the serial numbers have been removed. I'll take it with me in the morning and dispose of it out past Barbados jurisdiction in international waters. I've got another that shoots the same and I'll leave it with you."

"You don't think his body was incinerated when the sedan crashed and exploded when hitting the rocky limestone cliff on the way down?"

"Just a precaution on our part to be rid of the weapon. Keep the holster and I'll give you the new pistol before you leave for school. I brought extras over when bringing clothes and personal items for my stay here."

"My mom really teed off some bad people, didn't she?"

"Yep, she did and paid for it with her life. Don't let that happen to you."

"Not to worry, if someone's gunning for me, they'll have to come to the island where I'll be ready."

Godwin realized then he'd have to train David in his surveillance techniques. For the rest of his life, he'd need to be vigilant in his safety because of his mother and his own involvement with the CIA. And, Thomason wouldn't be in his position forever to sift through the info that poses danger to his family.

He'd reached clarity for his next step. He had to track Ming's son, Chang Bohai, who moved about throughout the world. The hit he posted on the dark web had an IP address from Beijing but that was no guarantee he was there. Yet, he needed to move fast and take him out before he realized Nelson didn't fulfill his contract and hire another mercenary for the job.

Confident he had maybe 24 hours to act, he left Lulu in charge admonishing her to not open the door to strangers.

He needed to return home and access his computer to locate Nelson's employer, Chang Bohai.

Since creating his new identity as Jim Godwin, he'd only been back to Beijing once and he'd stayed clear of his old associates. He was concerned his size and height would give him away. He wanted to make sure he had a strategic plan for locating and killing Ming's son, Chang Bohai, swiftly and be back on his flight to Barbados.

He'd heard whispers about a deadly virus spreading fast and furious in China. Unknown to the public now, he had a window of opportunity to act before a lock-down was ordered and air travel would be impossible.

He tracked Chang Bohai and found him working in a leadership role at a multinational financial services group. He hacked into his computer and scanned his calendar. Establishing the date of his trip, he gave himself 24 hours to be in and out of Beijing.

He ruled out the use of poisons, unlike one of his mother's favorite choices, and decided to hit him in his bank's parking garage. Although sounding easy, and quick enough, he wasn't sure of his martial arts abilities and counterattack potential or eyewitnesses.

He would buy what he needed to camouflage his own identify and not restrict his movement. Thinking over his options to expedite the kill, his attack would depend on how things played out in the garage notably if others were present or he was alone. He preferred to act under the cover of darkness with one clean kill shot.

When going into battle he was always confident he'd win. Yet, this time with the closeness he felt toward his son, he decided to leave a note warning him about Ming's son, Chang Bohai, if he didn't return.

His will was already prepared to gift David all his holdings. This had been done years ago when he realized he had a son. With the basics taken care of, he'd focus on the deadly job ahead.

CHAPTER NINETEEN

Unmasking the Future

G ABBY WAS RELAXING poolside with the Caribbean sun warming her body. Her daily swims were beginning to show results in her upper body strength and coordination and flexibility of her lower body, especially her legs.

Lulu had treated her from the scarring of her recent surgeries to heal the mangled tissue on her body. She believed her homeopathic medicine and herbal poultices did as well as the prescription ointments she'd brought from Italy.

By sunning with a high-quality sunscreen, Neutrogena Ultra Dry-Touch Sunscreen SPF 55, a little each day, the ugly marks from surgery were beginning to fade. She'd hoped to wear island clothing and a bathing suit when family and friends gathered for a relaxing evening on the terrace. Her mind quickly went to the towering Godwin always available when needed.

She was entranced by Godwin's gentle spirit when he was present. He'd taken David under his wing to teach him manly things she couldn't. He had a way about him that left her longing for someone she could never have-Walker. She wondered if she'd ever separate the two in her mind. For she'd like to learn more about him, for he made her laugh and if she read him right, he was interested in her as a woman.

She'd overheard he and David talking about women and found out he and Jenna had quit dating. Yet, no doubt, many beautiful island women would love to warm his bed. When he returned from his business trip to the United Kingdom, perhaps they'd have a shot at knowing one another better. But, how would David react to his auntie being involved with his friend and mentor?

She stopped herself and thought, back to basics, one foot in front of the other until the timing is right. Trust the process she reminded herself for the umpteenth time.

Her cell rang and she answered, "Hello, Thomason."

"How's my favorite lady today?"

"Getting better, thanks to you."

"Good to hear. I've got good news for you. The crispy fellow they pulled out of the ravine was your nemesis, Nelson. He'd leased the car under an alias, but his DNA was a match with his military records. That's one less murderer on the loose who'd likely targeted your son."

"Well, all I can say is his failure to negotiate Deadman's curve was paybacks for what he did to me and planned for my son."

"You've got that right. Now that you're on the mend, what are your plans? I realize you like to stay busy, but you can't practice or teach law - ever again. Understand?"

"Don't worry. I barely escaped with my life and wouldn't if not for you. My life as Sydney Jones is over and Gabrielle D'Agostino is not a lawyer and doesn't plan to become one."

"Thank you for setting my mind at ease. I'm just concerned you'll get bored and do something stupid. I know you're restless, I just want you to have something to occupy your time that'll not kill you."

"Don't be afraid, I've been thinking about that. Besides doing crossword puzzles to sharpen my mind, I've been doing a lot of reading, especially romance novels. I'm thinking of trying my hand at it after studying more about the craft to develop my writing style."

"You can't use the name you're going by now. Some hungry journalists may start digging and give you some unwanted publicity or divulge your location. Then there are possibilities you could attract a different kind, but still deadly stalker."

"You make it sound like I'll be writing murder mysteries. I promise that'll not be the case. I'll use a pen name and conceal my location. You worry too much. Take a breath and relax things are looking better than they've in a long time."

"Ok, keep me informed for I have the resources to provide you an authentic pen name that'll pass scrutiny."

"Thank you. I appreciate your help. But first I've got to learn how to write so there's no hurry."

"In the meantime, keep me updated on your progress health and otherwise."

"You've got it."

She hung up the phone knowing Thomason was one of the best friends she'd ever had, and she didn't want him to worry about her.

Christmas was fast approaching, and she had an idea. He'd probably be home alone or work for others to take off to be with their families. She decided to buy him a first-class open-ended ticket to Barbados as a gift. Secretly she'd love to see him during Christmas. She smiled.

.

CHAPTER TWENTY

Deadly Aim

G ODWIN CHECKED IN at his hotel on Beijing's Financial Street within walking distance to Ming's son's banking headquarters. He wasted no time double-checking his movement for the evening and the next morning on his computer. He'd prefer to strike after dark and would if he stayed late at his office. And, he was working late according to his appointment calendar creating an opportunity for a late-night hit. If he was alone when leaving, he'd hit him tonight and be done with the deed.

He walked to the nearby financial conglomerate's parking garage and pinpointed Chang Bohai's deluxe luxury automobile parked in the VIP section. He carefully picked a secret hiding place and waited. From his schedule, he knew it wouldn't be long before he came through the elevator doors and headed toward his car. That's when he'd pull his pistol with a silencer and fire then take his keys, and dump his body in his trunk. He ruled out physical force and a brutal bodily attack for he needed to be quick and gone immediately from the scene.

He waited for the chirping sound the car alarm system would make when he neared his automobile. He'd guess his finger would be on the button as soon as he stepped out of the elevator. He was right. In front of him was the man who'd contracted to kill Sydney and their son, David.

He aimed for the "apricot" or the medulla oblongata, located inside the head and fired using the double-tap shooting technique. He fired two shots in rapid succession between breaths using his semi-automatic pistol with a suppressor. Chang fell to the concrete slab of the garage. He quickly checked for a pulse and when finding none picked up his keys that'd fallen from his hand and pressed the trunk button. When it popped open, he lifted his body while still wearing gloves and dumped it into his trunk along with his car keys. Then slammed the trunk shut. Acting quickly and precisely, there wasn't a mess to clean up – a perfect CIA hit.

He looked around to check if anyone was nearby or exiting the elevator. He was in luck for the coast was clear. He removed his ski mask and jogged back to his hotel. He'd been able to carry out his business on his schedule and it wouldn't be long before he was sitting in first-class with bourbon in his hand for the long flight home.

ooooo

David was missing Godwin for they hung out daily either at his home sparring, doing tech stuff, or on his fishing boat. He wondered what business he had to take-off abruptly with things still up in the air with Nelson's employer for murder still at-large.

He headed home after school and found his Aunt Gabby downstairs watching the news. She was looking healthier and tanned; she'd turned into quite a beautiful woman since arriving. He was feeling better about his future knowing she'd recover from her ailments and he'd have family. He'd always love Daniela for all she'd done especially after his mother's passing. But she had her own family now, a new baby daughter to care for and raise.

Gabby's recovery had lifted a burden off her shoulder's where she could move next door and begin a new life with her husband and daughter, Mikaela. He wished them the best and was glad they continued their friendship with Gabby. Yet, she had to be bored now that she could move around without aid and wasn't tied to her reference – *dream home.*

○○○○○

Today, after school he entered their home through the garage door after parking his bike still leaving room for Godwin's in case, he returned earlier than expected. He walked through the living room after stopping off in the kitchen for a snack, and went out on the terrace. There he found Gabby doing the unexpected–shooting at a giant target at the other end of the terrace with a reverse limb crossbow known for its low cocking weight and impressive velocity.

He stopped short of her seeing him and watched as she pulled back the arrow past the threshold to aim and release. Her fingers were smooth as she notched her arrow. On release, the arrow flew directly into the center of the bullseye planting itself firmly into the target's surface from the rapid acceleration.

He needed to learn about his auntie. Apparently, there was more to her than he realized. To become a skilled archer, it took years of practice to be proficient with a crossbow. She had a deadly aim and he felt better about her safety knowing she was alone in their home when he was away at school, with friends, or Godwin.

He naturally wondered what she could do with a gun and if she'd ordered targets to practice with on the terrace. The money wouldn't be the problem, for she was loaded, if she wanted to build an indoor gun range on their massive property, she'd do it. And, after all, she had a life estate on the property with it returning to him in the event of her death. He was liking her more each minute.

He walked over to her and said, "Where did you learn to shoot a crossbow?"

In her silky Italian voice, she said, "At my estate in Tuscany, we often had competition for our staff and vine-yard workers. It kept life interesting. We'll have to go there one day and let you meet everyone and sample our private label. One day it'll be yours so learning about the business now would be helpful."

He loved the sound of her fluent Italian voice. She spoke like she was singing, and it sounded pretty. He wondered if she'd teach him the language, at least enough to not sound daffy when they visited the estate.

"Sounds good to me," he said. I've never been to Italy or was too young to remember the visit."

"You've been there but you're right you were a baby then. But I bet the staff would love to see you all grown up."

"You're kidding me?"

"No, I'm serious," she said. "The present staff has worked for my family for years. They are ready year-round for someone's visit to the estate. Plus, many of their family members work in the vineyard during the harvest season or in the winery."

○○○○○

"I can't wait to visit. Can I bring my friend Jason? He's never been off the island and has a sharp mind and inquisitive nature. I'm sure he'd love to learn more about being a vintner and take in different scenery."

"Yes, of course. We'll pick a time during your school vacation to visit and you can invite your friend with all expenses paid."

"I can't wait to tell him about our trip. He'll be stoked."

Gabby smiled. Glad to see her son happy for a change.

Godwin makes it to the airport with time to spare. He didn't want to be late boarding his flight back to Barbados away from the Chinese government's scrutiny. He felt the prick every time he'd entered the communist country wondering if one day he'd be delayed and questioned.

An agent he'd met years ago shared his story about their interrogation and trauma from surviving their merciless methods. While still working with the CIA, they'd met in the states and he'd said, post-traumatic stress disorder (PTSD) forced him into medical retirement from the company.

He'd been in and out as an agent many times with no problems. He just wanted to go home one more time for he had no plans to return. He was in luck. When his flight was called to board, he immediately made his way to the aisle. Never looking back or speaking even though he was fluent in Mandarin. He moved with the crowd toward the boarding gate.

He'd done this many times and hoped today was no exception. He noticed he was holding his breath and squeezed and released his fists in his pockets away from prying eyes and kept moving forward. Finally, he was boarded in first-class and immediately ordered a drink.

Now if the plane would lift off, he could relax and enjoy his bourbon on the rocks. The stewardess took them through the airlines required procedures in event of an emergency. He listened half-heartedly for he'd heard the same spill numerous times. Now, if they'd get strapped in and ready for take-off, he'd be happy. Minutes seemed like hours before he heard, this is your captain speaking...

Finally, he was on his way home. He was getting too old for this routine for what used to be second nature, now gave him pause especially with the rumors of a deadly virus. He couldn't wait to return to his island and family.

On landing, he went straight to his home first to check to see everything was as he left it – and it was. He got on his motorcycle and headed to David's home overlooking the Caribbean, not far from his abode. He parked in their garage and went around to the front door to ring the doorbell as a courtesy.

David opened the door and rushed to hug him. He wasn't surprised and hugged him back. "Miss me?"

"Yep, your business trip came out of thin air. I was worried about you and your sudden disappearance when we still have a murderer at-large."

"Not to worry, I heard from some higher-ups in the U.S. government that Nelson's employer met his demise. They're still investigating but that's the look of things. So, we can go about our daily lives without watching over our shoulders, at least not from an attack from him."

"You don't say? It's good you have friends in high places." David paused for a minute to collect his thoughts.

"Yep, that's true. So, what's for dinner tonight? Has Lulu made plans to cook, or do we have the honors?"

"Well, you're in for a surprise, actually more than one but that can wait to later. Gabby has dinner roasting in the oven–a turkey with dressing. She says she is practicing for Christmas dinner for when she expects a special friend to visit."

"Well, I for one don't mind being a guinea pig for a good cause." He laughed and David joined in for once good things were working out for his family.

Gabby was an amazing hostess and even Godwin was impressed with her way around the kitchen. She's said with time on her hands, she found exploring food recipes and cooking was therapeutic.

The evening was relaxing, and everyone enjoyed Gabby's dinner or at least said they did. Afterward, she made drinks for herself and Godwin and asked if he planned to stay the night. She recognized he'd just returned home from the UK and probably wanted to turn in early. He was welcome to crash with them. In fact, his presence put both her and David at ease.

Godwin thanked her for her hospitality and said, "I'd love to stay the night. Your company is a lot better than my going home to an empty house."

Gabby smiled and said, "Make yourself at home. I'll see you in the morning."

She took the elevator to her upstairs bedroom suite and left Godwin and David downstairs to chat.

David said, "You won't believe the changes I've seen in Gabby, just since you left for your overnight trip."

"You don't say. Tell me about it."

The inquisitive look on Godwin's face left him no choice but fill him in on his aunt's magnificent recovery. Although, to be honest, she'd been taking care of herself with Lulu's help since she arrived. The results he'd seen in her physical condition was amazing. She no longer crept around like an old woman and even to him, she'd became beautiful in a serene Italian kind of way.

David couldn't wait to tell him about her skills as an archer and an invitation to her Tuscany estate. He gave him the lowdown about his discoveries. Godwin was surprised too. Instinct told him there was more to Gabby than first impressions. Now he was certain.

He couldn't shake the déjà vu feeling he had when she was near. He couldn't get past thinking of Sydney when in her presence. She was beautiful and as David said, had grown even more so since recovering from her ailments. He wanted to know more about her and the mystery guest she was expecting for Christmas dinner. He wondered if he could wrangle an invitation. He hoped so for he'd love to spend Christmas with his son and learn more about Gabby.

CHAPTER TWENTY-ONE

Holiday Surprise

G ABBY WAS UP early and downstairs to send David off for school. Something she'd been wanting to do since arriving. A flashback of their mornings before the life-altering attempt on her life came to mind. And, she smiled when he looked up from his cereal bowl as she made her coffee and sat in the chair across from him.

She realized now the past rapport with him was gone when told his mother died. But she'd make the best of it. Something was better than nothing and perhaps they could create a new relationship. She hoped so.

Thomason was right, she'd never want to go back to practicing law for the business had robbed her of being David's mother. Whatever she chose to do wouldn't affect her family life with her son. That she'd promise herself.

She said, goodbye to David and went out on the terrace to practice her Tai Chi. She'd taught David the art when he was very young, and she was glad he'd returned to it since being on the island. She'd watched from her upstairs window early in the morning while he went through his routine before breakfast. She wished they could practice together again.

Sitting on the terrace enjoying the Caribbean view, her cell rang, it was Thomason. She smiled.

"So, you want a houseguest for the Christmas holidays?" he asked.

"Yes, I've invited a very dear friend and hope he will accept my offer of a Caribbean Christmas on the island."

"You, don't say."

"Yes, can you make it?"

"Yes, I wouldn't miss it for the world."

"Well, consider yourself penciled in." She laughed.

"So how are things in the states? Still catching the bad guys?"

"Yes, another reason for my call, our investigators determined the hit on you was initiated by Ming's son, Chang Bohai. He used the dark web and Nelson to carry out his plans. He also marked David for death. Nelson was in Barbados following his leads from overtaking Judith's affairs and discovered his contract for kill notice.

"So, is David safe now? Has he been arrested and charged with my murder?"

"Don't you fret. Chang Bohai is dead. He was murdered in what appeared to be a CIA hit, but between us, the Chinese government is saying he'd brokered a financial deal that went bad."

"And, when did this happen?"

"Just yesterday or I'd called you sooner."

"Thanks for calling to tell me my son is safe from that lunatic."

"I'll arrive the week before Christmas. Is there anything special you want for Christmas?"

"Just your friendly face is enough. I can't wait."

"Same here."

Gabby ended the call and thought about recent events. Strange as it seemed, Godwin's 24-hour business trip coincided with what Thomason told her about Chang Bohai's murder. She'd love to peek at his passport and learn where he was yesterday. She wondered if he left his passport in his nightstand beside his bed downstairs. And, should she look while he was away?

ооооо

Godwin and his business partner, Alex, were busy gearing up for the peak charter fishing season, January through April when all the game fish are in season. Reservations were rolling in above average from the previous year already.

He was tempted to buy another salt-water vessel and expand their holdings. The younger set, David's age and older, liked to charter luxury salt-water vessels to tour the island, swim, and water-ski. From the latest boat show, he attended in Ft. Lauderdale FL he was convinced the perfect line for that demographic's enjoyment, was the *Monterey*, a keen sports boat for fun and games on the water.

He and Alex talked and agreed to investigate the possibilities. Next, was to find a captain and crew to outfit the venture. David would be perfect for making sure the guests had a good time enjoying watersports. But he didn't want to tie him down since his friendships were important and he was learning family first now that Gabby was beginning to enjoy leaving home and shopping and dining downtown.

He'd not intrude on his plans by suggesting he work unless he wanted to on some charters when he wasn't doing anything else. Perhaps it could be something he and his friend, Jason, could do together for both to earn some extra money. He likes the fact that although David was wealthy from the inheritance left by his mother, he was a hustler, wanting to find new ways to earn money.

After the meeting with Alex, he returned home to wait for David. Then afterward, he'd follow him home and stay the night at their home. Spending time there had become second nature and he was beginning to understand Gabby better.

She reminded him of Sydney and he almost kissed her when they were playing around in the kitchen one evening making dinner. He was glad he'd caught himself. He still needed to be careful with females although he'd admit to being attracted to Gabby. Darn it - if she didn't remind him of Sydney, he'd express his interest or maybe that was the attraction to her.

He couldn't get her out of his mind and the act of pursuing her was complicated. They'd have to be ground rules, for a CIA hitman might show up at his front door.

Slow and easy would be his mantra. He'd explain his situation in a dubious way leaving out the deadly details. He'd given it much thought and believed they'd be fine on the island if he paid attention to their surroundings. Going to the states was out of the question, too much risk involved. However, hearing about a possible trip to Tuscany and he was all in.

They'd be safe around people she'd known all her life. He was waiting for her to ask for his companionship in Tuscany. Thinking of out of country travel, he remembered one of his passports was in the drawer on the bedside table at Gabby and David's. He'd not want to explain his deceit about where he'd been to Gabby. Hopefully, she was too busy with her Christmas planning to question his whereabouts.

He used an alias when he wanted to separate his new identity for safety precautions. The passport left behind was one of them. He'd put it in his backpack tonight for prying eyes didn't need to learn more about him. He hoped Lulu didn't clean in his suite today and find it or Gabby go on an expedition to fuel her suspicions. She had them for he'd been a spy long enough to recognize when someone was holding something back, they wanted to be kept a secret.

He worked on some tech proposals for companies he represented who wanted to up-the-stakes for their digital security. He'd just hit the send button on his computer when he heard David parking his bike out-front. He met him at the door and said, "Come in. I've been waiting for you."

"Am I in trouble, what's gives?"

"No, not unless you're holding out on me. Grab a drink from the frig and tell me about your day."

"Ah, same old stuff, different day. Not much going on for everyone is in the Christmas spirit. The teachers are as ready for a break as the students."

"If you can make it to the end of the week, you'll be out for a spell."

"I'm ready. I'm looking forward to Gabby's mystery guest. She's gone crazy decorating the house for the holidays. I haven't seen her this happy since she arrived. This Thomason guy must be a special friend."

"What did you say his name was?"

"Thomason an old friend she'd met in Atlanta when mother was alive."

Godwin felt like choking. He coughed and stood up to get a drink of water from the kitchen faucet.

"Are you alright?"

"Yep, just needed a drink to clear my throat."

When Godwin returned to the kitchen table, he asked: "Have you met him?"

"No, I don't believe I've had the pleasure."

"Well, you will in a couple of days. Gabby's driving to the airport to pick him up herself although I offered."

"I suppose we'll meet him together then."

They chatted about fishing and wondered if Thomason would enjoy some fresh fish during his stay. He could grill them on the terrace while Gabby caught up with news from her friend. He'd ask after dinner tonight if he and David needed to make fishing plans.

"He might enjoy catching some Yellowfin or Wahoo himself," said David. "That'd make his vacation memorable, don't you think?"

"We'll ask Gabby if we can borrow her friend for a while."

"She'll not mind and probably like the idea if it helps her friend enjoy his stay."

"We can make a suggestion and plan accordingly."

They went downstairs to the gym and did a short 45-minute workout before heading home. He was glad David's interest remained robust for building his strength. Carrying the Jones name and being the son of a burned spy, he needed to stay in top form.

They straddled their bikes and took off with David in the lead headed home. As they rode around Deadman's curve, Godwin peered over the ravine where Nelson's car exploded. He was grateful his son was an excellent rider and acted forcefully when threatened.

CHAPTER TWENTY-TWO

To Live Again

NO MORE MOPING around the house. Gabby now arose early to see David off to school and do her calisthenics and swimming to begin her day. She was reading more and studying the craft of writing. The idea of writing her own romance novel was taking form and gave her something to occupy her time.

She'd decorated their home for Christmas and couldn't wait to pick up Thomason from the airport in her sportscar. They had a lot of catching up to do. He was the only person she could talk to about her son and the feelings of loss as his mother. He'd be pleased they were developing a special relationship, not as mother and son, but family.

She'd done some snooping in Godwin's bedroom suite after thinking about the coincidence of his business trip to the UK and the death of the employer of Nelson, her targeted assassin. He'd left his passport in the drawer, and she was surprised when looking at a different name than the one he used on the island. The passport was stamped when entering and exiting Beijing China. The timing was right on. There was more to this man than what he'd revealed. But what?

She'd love to talk with Thomason about what she found even though it was only a theory. Her concern was he'd get others involved and if Godwin was in trouble expose him. If he was the hitman responsible for killing the man torturing her family, so be it.

Maybe one day Godwin himself would tell her the story. He'd always had a connection to David that's why she'd encouraged Daniela in her final papers to treat him as a family for David's sake.

There'd been always something about this man that pulled her to him, what she couldn't explain. But she was willing for the story to unfold in its own timing.

It wasn't long before David and Godwin were coming through the garage door each shedding their motorcycle jackets and hanging them on the rack in the hallway. They were smiling as they greeted her.

"Nice to have you home. I've made our dinner, and we can eat early and enjoy the sunset over the Caribbean. What do you think?"

David said, "I'll leave the sunset gazing to you two. I just got a new game I want to play in the media room on the widescreen."

"Well you can set up your game while I put dinner on the table," said Gabby. "I'll call you when it's ready."

Godwin said, "Let me help you."

"Sure, I'll grab some plates and silverware from the cabinet and be ready for you to do the heavy lifting bringing the dishes to the table. We're eating family-style tonight with everyone helping themselves."

"Your cooking smells delicious," he said. "Is this another one of your dinners from your favorite celebrity cookbooks?"

"Matter-of-fact, yes! I've always wanted to learn French cooking and Jacques Pépin is the best in the world. He received France's highest order of merit."

"You don't say. Is this more practice for your holiday guest?"

"Lord no! He'd not be impressed at all. Cooking fish or BBQ on the grill is more his style."

"A manly man's dinner, huh?"

"Yes, if that what you call it. But I enjoy it as well."

"Whoops darn my stereotypes. I'm sorry."

"No need for many would agree with you."

"Just not you, right?"

"Well, if splitting hairs, yes!"

"I'll be more careful of my sexist comparisons in the future."

"I wouldn't expect anything different."

"I'm glad we aired that out, perhaps now we can call David for dinner." She smiled.

She used the intercom to alert David dinner was ready to be served. On entering, he graciously pulled back the dining table chair and waited for her to be seated. She thanked him.

He sat next to her and said, "Who's saying the blessing tonight?"

No one spoke up.

"Well, David," she said. "Why don't you?"

Within minutes, they were all sampling the French dishes Gabby had made both being equally surprised with her cooking skills. She was a good student and followed Jacque Pepin's instructions for making Chicken Jardinière served with crusty bread and Lemony Green Salad with Radicchio and Pepitas.

David was the first to excuse himself and said, "That was delicious Gabby. But, if you don't mind, I've got players waiting for my return to the game."

"No problem," said Gabby. "We've got the dishes and cleanup. Just don't stay up too late playing."

Good gosh, she thought, I sound like his mother. I hope he doesn't mind.

Godwin rose and pushed his chair under the table before walking over and pulling out Gabby's chair. He took the larger dishes and took them to the sink to load in the dishwasher while Gabby cleared the table.

The sequence of events brought back the Deja vu feeling of his life with Sydney. He couldn't shake it for it repeated itself every time he was around her. How could he ever become romantically involved with her when she reminded him of Sydney?

CHAPTER TWENTY-THREE

Forever My Love

G ABBY IS GIDDY with excitement knowing her friend
and confidant was arriving shortly. She dressed
early for meeting him. In minutes the top was down
on her sportscar, and she was on the way to the airport. She
smiles as the sea breeze teases her face remembering how
far she'd come. Listening to Thomason was the best thing
she'd ever done. Thanks to him she had a new life and was
reunited with her son.

She wanted his Christmas vacation to be special and
hoped he would go deep-sea fishing with her son and Godwin.
They'd have plenty of time to catch up during his stay.

Deep down she hoped he'd liked Godwin for she'd
elevated him to an important role in David's life. She was
thankful for his manly influence and help with raising him.

She recognized him immediately. You couldn't miss him
in the brightly multicolored tropical shirt he was wearing. He

must have ordered it off the Internet under the shopping category "Leisure Caribbean Wear." She laughed for she'd gifted him with native produced shirts for Christmas with authentic Bajan styling. God love him for he was in the vacation spirit.

She waved and he walked over to the car, and she got out to greet him. They hugged. "Glad you're here," she said.

"Likewise. He kissed her on the cheek."

She cranked her speed yellow Porsche, and they headed toward her home.

"Nice ride," he said.

"Yes, I got Jonathan to go to the docks and sign for and garage it at home before I got blown up."

"I bet you were excited to finally drive it."

"Yes! It was a defining moment in my recovery when I sat behind the driver's wheel for the first time."

"You look great."

"Only because of you and your watching over me."

"I'm glad you are safe and reunited with your son. How is that going?"

"I sound more like his mother each day, and he doesn't seem to mind. At least he's not verbalized it if he does. I think he's just glad to have a family he can claim as his own."

"Yes, I agree. What you did in making Daniela his guardian after your murder made our story stick. If not, the killer would have kept coming after you, if they thought you were alive. I'm aware of the downside - your son will never know you survived."

"I live with that thought every day of my life. As much as I want to be honest with my son, they could've gone after him in Atlanta if they thought I'd survived. Sydney Jones is better off dead for there are more scumbags to come after me, especially with the human trafficking perverts I put behind bars."

Thomason was getting more comfortable referring to her as Gabby rather than Sydney. She was taking on a more serene attitude towards life and it suited her. He said, "Gabby, everything is going to work out. And, I believe you'll have a long-time relationship with your son you can be proud of. I am the keeper of your secret identity and it will follow me into my grave. Rest easy, my friend."

Gabby pulled into the garage noticing that her son and Godwin were already at home with their bikes parked side by side.

"Well get ready to meet my son, and Godwin, an important person in his life."

"I can't wait."

"I think they're on the terrace we'll meet them after stashing your luggage."

Gabby showed Thomason to his downstairs bedroom suite and said, "You can change into your swimsuit if you'd like a dip in the pool before dinner. I'm making drinks at the terrace bar, what would you like to drink?

He answered, "Make me one of your rum cocktails. I've heard Barbados rums are some of the best in the world."

"Will do. I got you a box of Cohiba Cuban cigars. I thought you'd enjoy lighting one up. They're sitting on your nightstand."

"Thank you. I always wanted to smoke a premium cigar. Give me a minute to change clothes, and I'll be right out."

"We'll meet in a few minutes."

She followed the sounds of water splashing in the pool where David and Godwin were throwing a football from one end to the other.

"OK, guys. My friend is here and will be joining us soon."

"I wonder if he can chunk a football?" asked David.

"Perhaps, we need to cool it for a minute," said Godwin, "and meet our guest."

"OK, I can be as dignified as you," said David. He laughed.

Godwin smiled; "You can still be your cheerful self, so he'll be meeting the real you."

Gabby listened to their exchange and would've sworn it sounded like a father-son conversation. Perhaps, that's what they'd become, she thought. She wondered if Thomason would pick up on that. Likely, she thought, for not much got by him.

Godwin and David cooled down their game and leaned against the edge of the pool as Thomason walked out onto the terrace. The expression on his face said it all - awestruck. Like everyone who visited her home, the view overlooking the Caribbean was captivating, surely one of the best on the island.

Gabby introduced him to Godwin and David. She said, "You've met my nephew, David when he was much younger."

"Yes, I remember David from when he was baby," said Thomason. "Although, I have to say he's grown a bit since the last time we met." He chuckled and said, "Good to make your acquaintance again, David."

David looked confused for a moment. Then said, "I'm glad you're able to spend Christmas with us. I've never seen Gabby happier."

Thomason smiled and said, "I'm glad to be here."

Then Gabby said, "Meet Godwin, a friend of the family and charter book captain on the island."

"Nice to meet you," said Godwin. "I hope you'll go fishing with David and me during your stay."

"Sounds good to me," he said. He turned and winked at Gabby.

"Well, enjoy the pool until dinner," said Gabby. "I'm sure Godwin has the grill fired up and ready for cooking one of his specialties."

The scent of apples coming from the Mulberry Smoking Wood Godwin was using to grill sent a tantalizing smell over the terrace. The ocean breeze whipped the scent of the natural growing Frangipani flower adding a delicate soft gardenia-like aroma to the air.

Thomason leaned back in his lounge chair, closing his eyes for a moment and enjoyed a drag from his Cuban cigar and sipped his Extra Old Fashioned made with Mount Gay XO. Gabby picked up on his whiskey cocktail preferences and mixed a perfect drink for the island made from a Barbados rum aged for at least 8 years in oak bourbon barrels.

He tried to keep his mind from wandering, but couldn't for this was the end goal for Sydney Jones, and he was a part of it. He was at peace for the first time in a long time.

Godwin dreaded getting out of the pool knowing his height and bulk would remind Thomason of Walker. But it was time to grill the Red Snapper and Caribbean-style Corn on the Cob for dinner. He eased up the steps of the pool ladder and grabbed a nearby oversized beach towel he'd left close to cover himself to walk to the cabana and change.

He reminded himself there was nothing else about him like Walker. He smiled as he walked past Gabby and Thomason. He breathed a sigh of relief as he quickly showered and changed clothes. There was too much that had happened recently for Thomason to get any ideas about him and start searching for more. Then, there was David. He'd handled the fight or be killed by Duane Nelson well, especially never having to kill a man before. The report of his death was ruled accidental and he and David would keep their secret forever.

He walked back to the terrace as if nothing was out of the ordinary and grilled dinner to everyone's delight and then invited Thomason salt-water fishing the next day.

He woke up early and went to the kitchen for a drink wishing for a Bajan style Bloody Mary for as long as Thomason was there, he was on edge. He wasn't surprised David was up and having his daily oversized breakfast.

"Are you ready to take Thomason out to our favorite fishing hole?"

"Yeah," he said and looked over his shoulder before continuing. "I think he's a cop. Am I safe around him after Deadman's curve?"

"You are completely safe. Even if Thomason learned the truth about what happened, he'd probably high-five you. He was your mother's number one fan. As long as he lives, he has your back."

"Whew, that takes a load off."

He was glad David was relieved for he was on pins and needles wondering if Thomason would find him out. His secret needed to stay that way for the CIA wouldn't stop if the word was, he was alive.

When Thomason came in from having early morning coffee on the terrace. Godwin said, "Let's take my jeep to the dock so we can all ride together. It'll only take a minute to ride home and get it."

"Sounds good to me," said Thomason.

David, high-fived him and said, "Yeah, we need plenty of room to bring home the fish we catch today."

Godwin was pleased with his plan for he didn't want any alone time with Thomason for him to ask questions.

In no time he returned and said, "Let's load up. The *Eclipse* is fueled and ready-to-go and daylight is burning.

They arrived at the dock and David quickly started untying the lines anchoring the boat while Godwin prepared for the cast-off from the harbor.

Thomason took a seat and observed as David and Godwin worked in tandem to ready the boat for their deep-sea fishing trip. He studied their similarity in movement and mannerisms. Although Godwin's speech and the overall look was different than Walker's, he felt certain he was one and the same man. And, David was his spitting image of the younger Walker. He wondered if Gabby was aware, Then, again, if she learned, she'd confided in him.

The family secrets and the end-run the CIA did on Walker to force him into their black ops were safe with him. He suspected when it was over, they'd put a hit out on him. Thence the change in name and physical appearance. He wondered if fate was what brought Gabby and Godwin to the island. He couldn't wait until the story unfolded. He'd sleep better at night knowing someone on the island was watching over her.

Godwin secretly hoped the sailfish were hungry today and Thomason would snag one for the record. He and David would concentrate on filling the cooler with Mahi Mahi or Red Snapper for dinner.

Thomason hooked a Blue Marlin and it put up a fight he'd long remember. When he finally reeled him in, he was tired but was wearing a big smile.

"Do you want to leave your catch with our taxidermy and have him mounted?" asked Godwin.

"Yes, I believe I will," he said. "I'll hang him on my living room wall for bragging rights and memory of this trip."

Godwin smiled. "OK, then I'll take care of getting the work done and the mount shipped to you."

David chirped up and said, "I think we've got enough fish to pay for our trip and then some. Plus, we'll have plenty for dinner tonight."

"I'll call Chef Ayato who wanted the Mahi Mahi and sell them when we dock," said Godwin. We'll clean ours at the wharf and they'll be ready to grill tonight."

ooooo

Christmas day everyone was up early and having coffee while gazing at the sun coming up over the Caribbean. David had already torn through the Christmas wrappings to uncover his presents. He was the happiest Gabby had seen him since arriving. She smiled thinking her presence played a role in his relaxed mood.

She went to the kitchen to check on the table arrangement and to pull the turkey from the oven where it had been cooking overnight on low heat. Godwin followed her and lifted the turkey from the oven and prepared to carve it for dinner. Gabby busied herself with placing the fruits and vegetables and desserts on the bar for everyone to help themselves.

David was in the media room playing his latest game with sounds of laughter spilling over as he gamed with friends. Thomason was poolside his favorite spot since arriving. She'd be sad when he left for home the next day.

When everything was ready to be served, she called David on the intercom and walked outdoors to tell Thomason that dinner was ready. He took her hand and with tears in his eyes, he said, "You have no idea how much this means to me."

She gave him a minute to wipe the tears from his eyes and said, "The feeling is mutual. I have enjoyed our visit and expect you to visit more often in the future."

"I'd have it no other way. You're like the family I never had."

"Ditto."

They ate dinner after Gabby blessed the food and gave thanks for the presence of friends and family. After cleaning up, Godwin left for the docks to check on his boat and things at home. Later he would return for dinner on the terrace for Thomason's last night on the island. She was glad he was staying the night again. His presence comforted her especially knowing her best friend was returning to the states in the morning.

Gabby toasted Thomason safe travel to the U.S. and hugged him. They were both teary-eyed. Godwin and David excused themselves and went inside to allow for their private moments. After a long day, each turned in early. At sunrise, the villa was stirring with everyone making coffee or something stronger to begin their new day.

Godwin said goodbye to Thomason and said, "I hope you'll visit again soon, and we'll take you scuba-diving off the reefs. We'll look for some sunken treasures."

"Thanks for asking. I look forward to it and getting certified will give me something to do in my off-time in Atlanta."

"Then, it's a plan. Godspeed home."

David entered the kitchen as Godwin was going out of the garage door. He was still sleepy from staying up late gaming with his friends. Yet, he realized today was a big day for Gabby since her friend was leaving. He decided to stick around the house in case she wanted to talk later.

He loaded Thomason's suitcase into Gabby's sportscar and said goodbye to him. "Gabby, I'll be here when you return. Take your time and enjoy the ride home."

She walked over and kissed the top of his head, "Thank you, David."

She and Thomason left for the airport and he went outside to begin his day by practicing Tai Chi. This was the most relaxing part of the day for him. Later, he'd make a sandwich from the turkey meat leftover from Christmas dinner.

Gabby drove Thomason to the airport. He said, "Gabby you don't need to go inside to wait for my plane. We can say goodbye here."

"Promise me you'll return for the summer break. When it gets steaming hot in Atlanta remember we have a nice sea breeze here and you're more than welcome to stay."

"I look forward to seeing you this summer. My boss will be surprised by my taking vacations back-to-back after nearly thirty years of service with no breaks to speak of."

"Maybe it's time to turn in your badge and relocate to a tropical setting. You have family and friends here."

"Definitely something to think about in planning for the future."

She smiled, and they hugged. Then he walked into the airport turning once to wave goodbye.

Gabby wasn't ready to go home right away. She needed time to think. Thomason moving to the island would be wonderful if that was what he really wanted to do.

He'd need more privacy than her sometimes loud home allowed. She'd wait for his directive and then once he arrived for his summer vacations, she'd have homes lined up for him to consider. Money wasn't a problem and she owed him her life. This was a minor offering compared to his gift of a new life. Perhaps when the time was right, he'd find a woman that would love him as she'd always loved Walker?

She stopped off in a downtown café for lunch and to settle her nerves before facing David. He was instinctive and had probably picked up that she and Thomason were old friends, unlike his auntie from Italy meeting him when he was a baby.

On the surface it sounded plausible but when you added their depth of emotions - it was a bust. She was certain David and Godwin didn't believe their story. She planned to play dumb for the moment. When asked specifics she and Thomason would discuss the options then reply as needed. In the meantime, she was studying the craft of writing and was getting ready to pen her first romance novel.

After reconciling her thoughts, she drove home to enjoy her son and the awe-inspiring Caribbean view. When entering the villa, she heard laughter from the terrace and realized David had his friends over for a swim. Great, she'd slip up to her bedroom suite after greeting them.

She needed to rest for the evening for Daniela's family was coming over for dinner. She'd sent over their Christmas gifts early to unwrap Christmas morning. She couldn't wait to see their reactions.

Godwin had promised to grill on the terrace, and she looked forward to his return. His choices for dinner would be exciting for he was resourceful in finding new grilling ideas. For now, she'd sleep.

Gabby awoke knowing she'd slept longer than intended. She washed her face and applied makeup before going downstairs. When the elevator arrived on the first floor and opened, she heard Godwin and David talking. Should she hesitate before making herself known? She listened.

She overheard them talking and discovered both were onto her and Thomason's relationship. She heard David say, "I'm telling you there's more to their relationship than is obvious, they're hiding secrets about their past."

"You may be right. But perhaps Gabby is overzealous in her recovery and wanted everything to be fine in your mother's memory? Afterall Thomason was her best friend."

"Well, just remember I told you so."

"Does it change anything about the way you feel about either of them?"

"Well, no but I dislike secrets that may affect me."

"At this point, I don't believe it to be life-threatening. So, can we give them the benefit of the doubt?"

"Yes, for now."

"Then, we'll cool it for everyone's sake."

"I'll stand down. The truth always has a way of coming out whether we like it or not. I can wait!"

Gabby waited a few minutes before entering giving them time to change the topic. She said, hello guys, sorry for my delay in coming down. I was exhausted after my day in town after dropping off Thomason at the airport. I hope you both like what I found today in one of the boutique shops. I couldn't help myself they were so manly and new surfing gear to the island."

They both chimed in, "You shouldn't!"

David said, "Christmas was over-the-top, and we are clueless about what you like to repay your kindness."

"Joining me for a trip home to Tuscany would make me happy. What about now while school is closed for Christmas break?"

"Wow," said David. "When are we leaving?"

"I've booked first-class for the four of us for the day after tomorrow. Can you squeeze that into your schedule?"

"I'll call Jason now and tell him to pack for our trip."

David left for his bedroom and to call his friend. Godwin stood still thankful that he'd been invited to her home in Tuscany. Yet, paying his own way was his choice. What should he say - thank you?"

He didn't want her to think he was a muncher. "Gabby, I appreciate the invitation for I'd love to tour Italy as only a native can show you. But, I'm not broke."

"I'm aware you can pay for the trip! Please let me treat you and show you my ancestral home? You've done so much for David and me, let me do this. Plus, you can help me keep an eye out for David and Jason. They'll be keen to explore the city and backup is appreciated."

He smiled knowing she was covering the bases. David was trustworthy but he wasn't grown up yet. "Let's just hope he and Jason don't plan on sowing their oats all at one time."

ooooo

Gabby had kept in close contact with the overseer at the Tuscany estate and explained she was bringing her young nephew and friend for a visit and wanted them to have a good time, but be supervised when in town. He had agreed that the estate would handle the surveillance of her nephew and friend during their stay.

After discussing the plans with Godwin, she left for her upstairs bedroom suite after saying good night.

Hours later, she was sleepless and went downstairs to the kitchen to get a snack. Although, she had a refrigerator in her bedroom suite stocked to overflowing with drinks. She was restless and wanted more but what?

She awakened Godwin for he was a light sleeper. He walked into the kitchen where she was standing. The light coverup over her nightgown left little to the imagination. Every emotion in his body exploded looking at her. Was he in a dream, and was Sydney in front of him?

What was he doing? He couldn't do this to Gabby - wanting to make love to her because she reminded him of Sydney.

She didn't say a word. With her finger over her lips to shhh him, she pointed toward the stairs, rather than the elevator whereby anyone awake would hear its movement. He tipped toed behind her like a lost pup wanting a home. The way she climbed the stairs was inherent to Sydney's athletic ability arriving at her suite in minutes.

They hurried into her suite and started kissing as soon as the door was closed. He pushed her onto the luxurious bed just before shucking off his clothes. She moved with him on the bed and was daring him to fulfill her.

He held himself back wanting to separate his desire for Sydney to Gabby. She wouldn't let him for she was hungry to be satisfied. He wanted to slow down to remember this as lovemaking to Gabby. He needed to separate them for his own wellbeing and anything in their future.

He touched her, and her skin responded to his fingertips just like Sydney's. He moved his hands over her body and instantly realized Gabby had been burned to the pulp.

He'd seen it in the war zone, bodies badly burned past recognition and others who didn't make it. He ran his fingers over the scars and realized she was a survivor. He tried to slow their lovemaking down to drink in the spirit of her body.

Gabby relaxed against his touch. This woman deserved his very best. She'd been through hell and lived. He wanted to take her to the top of the cliff in lovemaking and let her climax and come down on her own free will.

Now, if only the memories of Sydney would vacate his mind. But, he couldn't! *My God! He was making love to Sydney.* Every fiber of his being recognized her. This was not Déjà vu it was the real thing! Oh My God!

He dove deep penetrating everything that had gone on since they'd met trying to make it right. They were saturated in sweat and experienced a holy union and realized all past sins were forgiven. The future was theirs together.

CHAPTER TWENTY-FOUR

Second Chance

REATHLESS AND STILL feeling euphoric, Godwin lay beside Gabby with one arm holding her. He gently kissed her lips and wanted to pleasure her more. But, now wasn't the time, he couldn't spend the night in her suite. David was on the same floor and might notice he was there in the morning. He already had questions, and he didn't want to alarm him. He and Gabby would discuss strategies later.

Godwin said, "I know you're Sydney and your secret is safe with me. I've always loved you and only wanted the best for you. We have much to talk about since we were last together. I need to leave and go back to my bedroom, so David doesn't find us together."

Tears rolled down Gabby's cheeks, and she said, "I never believed it was possible for us to be together again. I believed you were dead but now I know you're not. You're right, we need to talk about what happened between us and decide what we'll tell David. I fear he'll be angry if he finds out the truth about both of us."

"You're probably right, and he already has suspicions about you."

"We'll deal with it tomorrow and then leave for Tuscany where he'll be busy with his friend, Jason, and we can decide how we'll handle our relationship and not devastate him."

Godwin tiptoed down the stairs to his bedroom stopping off in the kitchen to get bottled water. When he leaned his head against his pillow he was in shock. Gabby had a big secret, and he wished she'd confide in him. She was probably feeling the same way about him now.

His concern was for David and his reaction if he learned Gabby was his mother and him his father. He hadn't been rebellious in the past, but the hurt from the deceit surrounding him might overload his capacity to think straight.

ooooo

The next morning, he was up at dawn and swam laps in the pool to release the pent-up frustrations. Gabby would awaken soon and be down for coffee and her early morning routine of Tai Chi on the terrace. David would follow for his usual workout. By the time the house awakened he wanted to be in control of his emotions. If not, David would discern something had happened last night.

He decided to go home and pack for their trip to Tuscany. He'd called Alex to meet him at the wharf to go over the business before he left. He wished he had someone to confide in but, these were the secrets he'd killed to keep quiet. When he and Gabby arrived in Tuscany and were settled perhaps then they could talk.

"How's it going, man," asked Alex.

"It's all good," he said.

"So, you're going away for a couple of weeks with your lady friend and her son, good for you."

"Yes, I needed a scenic diversion." Then laughed at the pout on Alex's face.

"The business looks good and it appears we have plenty of deckhands for the charters."

"You're right, I've got this. Go have fun in Italy."

"That's my plan. Take care and I'll bring you a surprise back."

"Now, you're talking. Hope it comes in a bottle." He smiled.

"Yep, my kind of gifting."

Godwin returned home and looked over his technology business to be assured it was running smoothly. He'd take his laptop in case he needed to adjust anything while gone. Believing he had packed what he needed, he locked the door and left for Gabby's.

CHAPTER TWENTY-FIVE

Unsettling News

GABBY AWAKENED AND wondered if she'd dreamed of being in Godwin's arms last night. It seemed the universe conspired to unite them. Now, their secret identities were known by the other and without saying a word. The spiritual connection was made from a greater force outside of them – a Godly mystical intervention.

They did have much to discuss and waiting until their arrival at Tuscany seemed a lifetime away. But, they must for David's sake. She didn't want to lose her son again and feared if he knew the whole truth he'd panic and do something out of character.

She planned to talk to Thomason when she had clarity about their situation. But, would his knowing Godwin's identity subject him to danger if he let something slip? Or, perhaps with the exceptional detective skills he already knew and was waiting for her discovery of his identity?

She made her morning coffee, Dawn Patrol, and went out on the terrace to relax and watch the ocean waves lift and then crash into the shallow waters.

She'd found the note Godwin posted to the frig saying he'd be back shortly after packing for their trip. She waited for David to eat his breakfast and come out and sit with her before his workout. She needed him to be excited about his next adventure and not worry about household changes and family secrets.

Tomorrow they'd leave for the airport early to make their flight. She'd already decided Godwin's bedroom would be next to hers at the estate, the one Thomason used to be near when she was recovering from the attempted murder on her life.

Her womanly desires peaked with interest, knowing soon they could be together all night long away from the eyes and ears of family and staff. She couldn't wait.

ooooo

David's excitement for their vacation was contagious. His friend Jason was spending the night and ready to catch their flight to Tuscany. They were doing hush plans for their arrival. She was certain David had Googled the popular places to hang out in the region. She prayed they'd be safe and have a great time. In the back of her mind, she remembered making cautionary plans for their safety with the estate manager, and, relief washed over her body.

ooooo

Godwin returned with his bags packed and called a cab service with minivans to take the four to the airport. She doubted anyone would sleep that night from the excitement of a new adventure each in their own way.

Lulu made them one of their favorite Bajan dishes and she wished she'd agreed to go with them. Instead, she was taking her own vacation and returning home to be with family. She owed her for bridging the gap between modern medicine and homeopathic methods for healing her body. She wished her a relaxing time while they were away.

Early the next morning, the minibus arrived on time and they loaded their baggage and were on the way to the airport. The whole crew was quiet as the driver whipped through the streets unencumbered by traffic. When arriving Godwin paid the driver and lifted the bags from the taxi. Within minutes he was driving away to pick up his next fare.

ooooo

Godwin said, "Look alive boys and let's get these bags through security and ready to board our plane."

Although still sleepy from staying up all night and talking, they quickly picked up their bags while Godwin carried his and Gabby's and they easily boarded and were shown to their first-class seats.

Godwin softly touched Gabby's hand and she sat next to him. The boys were seated across the aisle and in conversation. She looked at him through tear-stained eyes, and whispered, "thank you."

He nodded.

They dozed off until awakened by the flight attendant who was preparing them for landing. Godwin looked across at the boys and saw them sitting erect ready to land and begin their new adventure. Adolescence, Godwin thought. They may all be in for a surprise with what the two of them had concocted together.

A luxury automobile from the estate was waiting for their arrival to return them to the villa. After loading their bags, the driver took them directly to Gabby's Tuscany home.

After arriving Godwin and the boys toured the estate. A vintage label taste-testing was arranged at the winery overlooking the vineyard. The boys could sample the wine and be awed by what they considered a bold flavor.

They met the vintner and the crew charged with production and distribution. David introduced his friend Jason to the boys their age and asked what was there to do in the region.

They made plans for the following day and when he glanced toward Godwin for backup he nodded in agreement.

ooooo

The evening meal was an elaborate Italian feast. The entrée *Pheasant alla Fiorentina* – Roasted Pheasant was served with the dressing removed from the inside and plated beside the bird in gravy and garnished with sage leaves.

The boys were introduced to the age-old tradition, dating back to the 16th century of unsalted loaves of bread accompanying the dishes. Each region has its own mark on the flavorless at first bread until soaked in leftover juices left on the plate. The basket was empty after they dipped their pieces into the gravy.

From the look on the chef's face, he was pleased to have hearty appetites like Godwin, David, and Jason at the table.

Afterward, the boys hurried upstairs to begin their gaming they'd brought with them from Barbados. Godwin and Gabby vacated to their suites.

Gabby said, "Why don't you stay in my suite tonight, the boys are upstairs and will never know what happens down here."

"My thoughts, exactly," he said.

Gabby filled their wine glasses from the uncorked bottle on the bar in her suite and wondered if they should talk tonight or could it wait for another day. She was hungry to be held in Godwin's arms again.

Godwin came over and took the glass from her hand, and set it beside the bed. She knew he had the same thing in mind, tomorrow is a new day, and tonight is about us. She excused herself and went into her changing room and returned with a revealing floral nightgown covered by a silk robe. They'd catch up on details from their past another day. None of it mattered for they'd found their way back to one another not on their own but by a force greater than themselves.

Their night together made the wait until Tuscany after their initial meeting, worthwhile and worries free about David finding out. Gone were the days of wearing winter flannel gowns in Tuscany and sleeping alone. Her dream had come true.

Gabby and Godwin's evening were joyful as they reunited in every sense of the word. Waking up beside him made her thankful she'd lived through the murderous attempt on her life. She didn't want to move for he was still sleeping wearing a smile on his face.

She slowly eased off the bed to get something to drink from the refrigerator and to take a shower and dress for the day. They would likely be outside today, so she dressed for the rabid winter weather with wool pants and a chunky sweater with boots.

She was ready for the day and the talk she and Godwin would have after the boys left to explore the neighboring venues. David had made new friends quickly since arriving and welcomed Jason into their brotherhood. Jason spent his alone time with the vintner learning about wine-making. Looking in the future, she smiled. Wouldn't it be grand if David's friend became the master vintner for the estate? For he was someone he trusted.

Godwin awakened and said, "You let me sleep in, I must have needed the rest for I'm usually up before sunrise."

"Take your time. I'm going to the dining hall where the boys are likely eating breakfast. Come whenever you're ready. I want to talk to David for they probably planned to leave early to tour the sites in Tuscany. My estate manager is guiding their activities for our two weeks visit so, we can relax.

"Ok, I'll see you later."

Godwin got up and prepared for his day knowing it would be gut-wrenching to tell his story and listen to hers. He wished they could skip this and go on with the peaceful relationship they had now.

The good news was Gabby's personality was opposite of Sydney's. The ole Sydney would've wanted to know everything immediately and, then have an attitude about him and Isabella. He had no problem calling her by the name Gabby for she was relaxed yet showed spunk when needed, totally different than the fire-breathing lovable dragon from his past.

He decided to check his emails and phone calls before beginning the day with Gabby. Although he was confident Alex had their charter business under control, he was the sole proprietor in his technology business, for now, hoping David would want in after he graduated.

He made the call-backs as requested by his clients. Nothing big just some tweaks here and there were needed to up their websites. Then he returned a call from a US Senator who'd he done work for in the past with his personal business. Standing at his closet to grab a heavy jacket for him and Gabby's tour of the property, he stopped for the conversation caught him off guard.

The senator, Jackson, wanted him to increase his personal home's security. An unusual request although they'd met and immediately liked one another. He asked the reasons behind his request; in case someone had targeted him with a death threat.

Jackson replied, "This is in the strictest confidentiality for if it becomes known they'll be world-wide panic."

He could feel the adrenaline rush from his comments and realized he was speaking the truth, but what about?

Jackson said, "We've received a verifiable warning that the world will be under attack by a virus coming out of China. My family lives in Washington DC making us one of the first to be potentially attacked. I'd sleep better if you'd make my home impenetrable by hackers and physical intruders. Will you take this on immediately?"

"Yes, I'm in Tuscany now but I can review and update your security from here."

"Thank you, and remember this is hush-hush."

"No worries, I've got your back."

Godwin hung up his phone and opened his laptop to review the senator's home security. He made some additions that would smoke anyone tampering with his security. He wished they were home where he and David could work together on apps to counteract the hackers during this time. Hopefully, they had time for in less than two weeks they'd be home. Yet, he checked his security systems to make sure they were working properly. They were.

He hoped Gabby didn't pick up on his vibes, for Sydney was an ace at that. He needed to compose himself before meeting her for their tour of the estate.

The chatter he'd picked up six months earlier about the Chinese using germ warfare to decimate the world came to mind. The report said they'd cooked up a *Horseshoe Bat* virus in their P4 labs and released it into their homeland with the goal of spreading it throughout the world. This was unbelievable. Who would knowingly kill their countryman to take over the world? Yet, he surmised this biosafety lab was developing a vaccine to counteract the effects of the virus once it was released for specific purposes none of which were uniquely humanitarian.

It was a scary thought and no country was immune from this pandemic of catastrophic proportions. What about his family? Where was the safest place for them to be in the next few months or even years?

In Tuscany, there was free health care even to visitors in the country. How safe would they be secured at the villa, yet they had a non-family member, Jason, with them and his family would want him home. They could always fly him home alone.

What about Barbados for their lock-down instead of Italy? Sure, they had plenty of wine to drink with a vineyard and winery and plenty of food on-site, but that could come to a stop if things got bad enough over a prolonged period. Plus, he needed to be at home working on new security measures.

Barbados is an island and can close the airport and not allow ships to port. They have rum distilleries and no fear of running out of booze or fresh water. The deciding point for him was the ability to take the boat out and catch seafood for food and provide an outing for those locked-in. But, when should he have this discussion with Gabby and David?

God, he wanted their vacation to end and they'd just arrived. Not because it wasn't enjoyable, but preparations were needed for this viral outbreak, like stocking up on canned food, personal items including toilet paper, medicines for Gabby and more. He was walking a tightrope knowing he couldn't disclose this knowledge at the present.

He called Alex and told him to not take anyone on board with a fever or cough. Alex immediately picked up a crisis was approaching and asked why.

Godwin said, "I'm hearing a nasty flu-like virus has infected some tourist and I don't want you or our employees to get sick."

"You want me to take their temperatures before boarding?"

"It probably not hurt, but they could be asymptomatic and not showing the disease, and still infect the crew. What about you and the crew wearing bandanas around your nose and mouth?"

"I get the hint, there's a badass virus going around. We'll take care of things here. Are you still returning in two weeks?"

"Yep, that's the plan. Sorry I had to spring bad news on you today. Keep our conversation to yourself until I get more info to verify the rumors."

"Will do, thanks for the heads-up."

"You know it brother."

Now to act excited about the tour of the estate with the news he'd received. He wanted to learn more about Gabby and the family's history, particularly sensing those connections saved her life.

CHAPTER TWENTY-SIX

Seeking the Truth

B Y THE TIME, they'd strolled through the vineyards and had lunch on the veranda the discussion he'd pushed out of mind, was due to happen. Gabby had been patient and was nonchalant about learning the truth, on the surface. He hoped she'd believe he didn't murder Roxanne and intentionally leave her.

She opened with, "I'd like to understand what happened with Roxanne and why you wouldn't fight in court to be exonerated, and then vanished in the early morning while I was sleeping? You could have said goodbye, its been fun, or something to save me from anguish and my foolish actions to find you."

"First, I didn't murder Roxanne. I'd saved her if I'd arrived minutes before her attacker. She'd been texting and calling me about being her personal bodyguard and I'd said no. She didn't stop so I told her we'd meet the next morning. When I arrived, she'd bled out on the marble foyer. I called 911 from her house phone and left it off the hook for the emergency team to find her address and left the door open.

"My fingerprints were found at the crime scene for I checked her pulse and left fingerprints on the door for I didn't use gloves. The CIA immediately scooped down and said, I had a choice; they'd make the charges go away if I ran a special op for them, or see that I was found guilty of murder. The other requirement was that I was to have no contact with you ever again. I knew you'd want to fight for my release, but knowing their underhanded methods, believed I'd put you in danger if I stayed."

"Thank you for telling me, I thought you were innocent, I didn't understand why you left without telling me the truth."

"I couldn't, not because I didn't want to stay and fight, but it was fruitless. They'd have their way regardless of my or your wishes."

"Late at night and especially after finding out I was pregnant with David, I held on to those thoughts, believing something sinister happened to make you leave me without a word."

"Gabby, I'm sorry for abandoning you. And, I thank you for having our son knowing he wouldn't have a father."

He reached over and touched her hand and realized it was shaking. He wondered if they should continue the conversation another day about what happened to her in his absence.

"Why don't we wait until tomorrow to continue your side of the story? I can wait. What do you think?"

"Yes, we have current issues to deal with and need to discuss what we share with David."

"You're right; do we tell him we're in love and leave the background out of the discussion?"

"That would be the easiest way to deal with our relationship especially since we're uncertain about how he'll react to the news. I don't want him to hate me for lying and for him to relive my death over again. He may never speak to me again after learning the truth, even if I was doing it to keep him safe."

"If we look at what's in his best interest, I think we found it. We don't need to dredge up the past when he is finding his way in the world. The news will be shocking and could undercut the process you're making in building a new relationship."

"I agree. Let's move forward and if he should discover something amiss, and have questions, we'll deal with it then."

Godwin took her hand and kissed it and said, "Thank you for understanding I had our best interest at heart in leaving you."

"I understand, and although there's more I want to know about Isabella, we'll leave that for another day. The boys will return soon and want to eat. I need to talk with the chef and see what's on the menu tonight."

She got up to go to the kitchen and Godwin breathed a sigh of relief. Now, if he could get accurate info on the spread of the virus, he could make plans for the family."

He opened his computer and began searching for the latest global news. There was nothing about a virus epidemic that threatened the world. Could his sources be wrong?

He thought not and, in the end, the citizens of the US will learn the truth and protest about their lying government leaders; whose only thoughts were to protect them and make a fortune off stocks relating to it, insider trading at its best.

CHAPTER TWENTY-SEVEN

The Italian Connection

D AVID, JASON AND his new friends from the estate returned and were all hungry. Gabby arranged for an early dinner knowing the crew would be famished.

Godwin was amazed how the estate had kept pace with the outside world in selling their wines, yet within the gates, a sense of history and fortitude from the tight group of families working the vineyards through the years was something he'd not seen in his world.

In looking around the estate he determined they are now and have likely always been self-sufficient. If things went bad during this pandemic, they'd have shelter and food to eat, and wine to drink. The acres of land housed livestock of cows, chickens, and hogs. The kitchen was always open preparing food for the workers whether Gabby was in residence or not. Her dad had prepared for the family legacy to live on after his death as his mother had before him.

He was tempted for them to hunker down there rather than returning to Barbados. But he didn't have his equipment to tap into the relevant conversation that could mean life or death and he didn't want to return home without them.

Gabby was calling his name, to come for dinner. He shook off the impending gloom and walked into the stately dining hall where everyone was already seated ready to eat. He quickly took his seat and after grace was said by Gabby, they ate.

The next day David, Jason, and his friends were traveling to the capital of Tuscany, Florence, Italy by train. Gabby wanted to go and visit cultural sites like the Uffizi Gallery again and dine with a panoramic view of the Apennine mountains while enjoying *Ostriche grigliate e granita di kiwi*, grilled oysters and kiwi granita with a glass of excellent wine.

She felt it best to stay home and plan to tour the city on a Vespa another time. She was regaining strength, but she feared a setback if she extended herself without resting. Besides, David needed some space away from family and he knew better than act out. The most she expected from this trip was for him to return with a leather jacket made by a master craftsman.

As Gabby instructed, adult supervision from the estate oversaw their care. There were no worries for the young people accompanying them visited the city often and could show them a good time. And, they'd not be sewing wild oats, for they'd already been warned.

Gabby was accustomed to looking over her shoulder, and her instinct said her son did the same. Today it was warranted, for someone was trailing them. When the attendant the estate manager sent to monitor and protect David and friends returned, he sent a private message to Godwin's suite, to come to the winery.

Godwin immediately left to find out what was wrong, hoping David hadn't done something foolish to land him in police custody.

The estate manager quickly dismissed police problems but said, "I think your boy is in danger here."

My boy, he thought. How in the hell did he find out?

Godwin wiped his face with his kerchief, and said, "I have no idea who's tracking him, for to my knowledge all the family enemies are dead."

"We can help you," said the manager.

"Who is we," said Godwin.

"The Italian Mafia," he said.

"Where in the hell were you when Sydney was being tracked by a monster and killed? I'm to believe family ties will save David?"

"We knew you had her covered and couldn't chance a connection then. Now, the distance is created to monitor David without it reflecting back on us."

"I was dead to the world, so how did you think I could protect her?"

"We track everything related to this family. By the way, you did what was expected!"

"Does David know your and Gabby's real identity?"

"No, and we want to keep it that way. She's been through enough."

"Who do you think is trailing David?"

"Since Sydney is perceived dead, we believe it's the US CIA looking for recruits. Is there anything they could use to blackmail him into their clandestine ops?"

"I can't think of a secret they could be aware of. With Sydney and me both undeniably dead, they have nothing, and she never identified his father."

"They may be interested because he is her son, nothing more."

"Tell me where you picked up this chatter so when we return home, I can track from there."

"No problem, we'll send an encrypted email of the links we're following."

"Thank you, since we're talking honestly, I'm hearing rumors about a worldwide health crisis from a virus released in China. Are you aware of this and taking steps to lockdown the estate until this is over?"

"Yes, we were waiting to see what you'd do – stay or return to Barbados."

"I'm thinking the island is the best place for lockdown. Tourism will be shut down after I talk with the ministry."

"You're welcome to stay here under our protection for this is Gabby's estate."

"Thank you, but I think being able to cast-off from shore for fishing around the island will help David when cabin fever sets in."

He laughed. "You're right, he's full of energy, probably another reason the CIA wants to recruit him."

"Thanks for the update and knowing you can trust me."

"We've been following you a long time and are glad you and Gabby made peace with your past."

"Me, too, and we've decided David doesn't need to know."

"That's your call, not ours."

Godwin went back to his suite and waited for the email from the head of the Italian Mafia, the manager of Gabby's estate to determine if it was the CIA tracking, David.

In minutes, the email popped up and he linked to their website for updates. After reviewing their sources, he decided they were right; it was the CIA, but why? Then he remembered how they profiled new agents. David with no parents fit their needs. No one to offer sympathy to except an elderly aunt for he'd made sure that description was live in places it mattered. They didn't need to be looking closer at Gabby or they'd figure out the truth.

CHAPTER TWENTY-EIGHT

The Outbreak

GODWIN WAS EXCITED to pack his bag and leave for the airport to return home to Barbados. He was pleased David made new friends, likely life-long at the estate. He and Gabby were caught up in a whirlwind of renewing their relationship. There were still unanswered questions, by both, but they could wait.

He wanted to return home and get the family settled and stocked-up before the worst thing in recent history rained down on them. He'd already placed orders for mandatory supplies for their home. They'd be shipped in before anyone realized a problem existed. He needed Alex and Jonathan to also prepare themselves and their extended families for this epidemic.

He'd make an appointment with the Prime Minister of Barbados on his return. She'd listen and take the necessary actions to keep their island safe and afterward, quietly and cautiously warn other countries.

When they returned home, Lulu met them at the door. She'd returned early to enjoy some quiet time away from her family and the Caribbean view. On the stove was a Chicken Curry with the Bajan signature seasoning of earthy oniony, peppery taste ready to be served over rice with salt bread.

David was the first to dish his plate full of the spicy Bajan food and sat at the bar to enjoy his homecoming after giving Lulu a kiss on her cheek and offering his friend, Jason a plate.

He and Gabby rode the elevator to return her suitcases to her bedroom and enjoy a few minutes together before meeting everyone downstairs. They'd have to tell David soon they were a couple. Otherwise, he'd think they were deceiving him, which in hindsight they were.

He'd wait and talk with Gabby later after the family conference about the health crisis on the horizon. Hopefully, she'd understand he didn't want to repeat himself and would deal with individual concerns.

Starving after the flight, they helped themselves to Lulu's Chicken Curry and took their plates on the terrace overlooking the Caribbean.

"Lulu did well with our homecoming meal," she said.

"Yes, I couldn't help but notice David devouring his before stashing his suitcase from our trip."

"Well, at least he invited Jason to fix his plate before chowing down." She laughed.

"Gabby, I'm calling a family conference for there is something urgent that needs to be prepared for now. I hope you understand I'll answer any question I can afterward."

"Do you want David's friend Jason to hear this?"

"Yes, he needs to be informed to protect his family. No worries, I am talking to the ministry tomorrow morning and everyone on the island will be warned."

"Wow, from your hurried breathing, this must be big."

"Yes, I'm afraid so, my love."

"Then do what you think is best."

"Thank you for understanding."

The boys were in the media room playing games. Jason had called his parents and said it was late and he was staying over the night and would come home in the morning.

Godwin called everyone into the living room. The boys yanked their headsets off after he gently tapped David on the head and placed them on the table and joined Gabby in the living room.

"OK, what gives," said David. "Our friends are waiting for us to return to our game."

"I have something to say worth your attention. Listen carefully, and any questions, I'll answer afterward."

David folded his arms across his chest when realizing the news was bad and he would likely play a part.

After they were seated Godwin said, "It's been verified from reliable sources that a virus outbreak will consume the world. The germ warfare source is from China and there will be no country safe from its effects.

Many will die and preparation is needed now for survival. I'm talking to the head of state tomorrow to lockdown our island before it is exposed by tourists. I've ordered bulk supplies for our home to get us through this crisis. I chose the island to shelter for the airport and ports can be closed. Plus being in lockdown we can take the boat out and catch fish."

David said, "I understand your reasoning, did you consider Tuscany while we were there?"

"Yes, and it is self-sustainable, and they will be fine. But, it's not the ideal location for us. The estate manager is working on shelter in place options now. Once the gate is closed, no one is coming through. I felt we needed outside pursuits that only this place allowed, like fishing from the dock if the ocean was blockaded."

"What precisely do you want us to do?"

"Stay inside and wear a facemask if outside."

"Do we have the facemasks?"

"Yes, they should arrive tomorrow, and I ordered enough for our family and friends. Also, bandanas can be folded and used as well."

Lulu crosses herself and says, "Holy Mother of God be with us."

Jason chirped up and said, "I hope my family is in the friend category."

"Yes, Jason, your family is covered. But you need to tell your parents to stock up on canned food and personal items."

"Wow, this is like living in a horror movie. I wonder if my parents will believe me."

"I hope so, for once the word is out, there'll be a rush for food and products like toilet tissue, cleaning products, and canned goods."

Although it was late, Jason wanted to go home to warn his family. But, decided to get up early instead hoping Godwin would back up his story if needed.

CHAPTER TWENTY-NINE

Serious Business

G ODWIN DECIDED NOT to go to Gabby's bedroom suite for it was on the same level as David's. He said goodnight to all in the living room and went to his downstairs bedroom. As he was leaving, he saw David lean down and kiss Gabby's cheek and say, "Good night."

The boys went to David's suite, not stopping in the media room to play online with friends. Lulu walked out on the terrace likely to say more prayers before turning in for the night. She was concerned for her family and rightly so for they scraped by doing handy work.

The house was quiet for everyone was asleep. Godwin heard his doorknob turn and quickly grabbed his pistol from under his pillow. When the door opened it was Gabby standing clothed in her robe. He put the gun away and she tiptoed to his bed. A spark of memory from their first encounter flashed across his mind. They quietly made love and fell asleep with his arm wrapped around her.

The next morning, he awoke and made coffee while Gabby slipped up the stairs to her bedroom to change for the day. When she returned, they took their coffee mugs and lounged by the pool overlooking the Caribbean. They enjoyed the peace and the sound of the waves crashing against the shore.

When David and Jason awakened, they made breakfast and planned their day. David was taking Jason home for a while to give him a chance to talk with his parents about the outbreak likely headed their way.

David figured he and Godwin would work on technology projects and be prepared for an army of attackers during the crisis. He'd wait for his lead since he had appointments scheduled today with the Prime Minister and Alex. Until then he'd go about his daily routine and get in a few laps while waiting and talk to Gabby. He wondered how she was handling the news about a world-wide epidemic.

David returned home after dropping Jason off at home. He went to the terrace where Gabby and Lulu sat talking. Not to interrupt, he listened as they discussed plans for the next couple of months. All nonessential outside activities would be canceled and she planned to invite Daniela and her family for dinner so Godwin could explain the present state of the global health crisis.

David was excited about Gabby's fighting spirit. He feared she'd be overwhelmed and become depressed about something out of her control.

ooooo

Godwin left for his appointment in town and then later to the wharf for meeting Alex on the charter boat. He was ushered into the Prime Minister's office and she invited him to sit down. He thanked her for meeting on short notice and explained what he'd discovered and provided suggestions to curb the effects in Barbados.

She agreed with his assessments and asked how he learned about the disease for none of her sources had mentioned it. He referred to his technology business and his global clients who were vigilante in monitoring the world for events shaping their economy. In providing the details, he asked she treat him as a confidential source and refer to her ministry as staying on top of global news affecting their island. She agreed.

His next stop was at the docks with Alex. They had much to discuss and Alex needed to prepare his family for the disaster coming their way. He hoped his family and friends could stock up before the supplies ran out by shopping for small amounts, at different stores to not cause an outage of products everyone needed.

He was glad to see Alex and thank him for keeping the business running while he was in Tuscany. Alex welcomed him on board the *Eclipse* and handed him a rum drink. In return he gifted him with a fine bottle of wine from the estate in Tuscany.

He said, "Bro we've got some bad stuff headed our way and unfortunately it'll likely hit here during our top fishing months. It's too risky to get infected from tourists taking charters out."

"Whoa," said Alex. "So how are we to keep our business afloat if we can't take on charters?"

"Hopefully, before the season is over our charters will be running as usual. Our business is in good shape and we have money in the bank to make payroll for you and our regular deckhands until this is over. I also have a fund we can dig into if needed for emergencies."

"This is mind-blowing, right when our numbers are inching up every year for charters."

"I know what you mean. What do you think about our fishing and selling our catch at the docks to anyone as we sometimes do for restaurants?"

"Why not, we'll be providing a food source during a crisis," he said.

Godwin felt awful relaying the news for Alex was excited the charters already booked exceeded the past year. He said, "Let's wait for the Prime Minister's announcement before we cancel fishing trips. However, remember to wear your bandana as a face mask and gloves when tourists are on board."

"I'm with you on staying safe even if I do have to cancel charters already booked."

"We'll get through this together. For now, you probably need to check your home supplies and freezer and stock up for a couple of months, at least."

"I'm leaving for home now and then grocery shopping for necessities."

They quickly said, goodbye to finish their to-do lists.

He hoped they had an early start on a potential pandemic headed their way. Listening in on American spy agencies he learned in November 2019 data had been collected about a health crisis in Wuhan China. How long before it would reach the island, he couldn't calculate. But he had sounded the alarm for his fellow islanders.

He went by his home to check the sources he was following about the health crisis on his computer. He wondered if Gabby had talked with Thomason to learn about preparation in the States. Apparently, the virus wasn't being discussed at least on the news networks. Where were the investigative journalists when you needed them to cover something with the potential to affect the world?

He secured his home system to return to Gabby and David's. When he returned, Lulu was in the kitchen cooking one of her Caribbean specialties. He said hello, and dropped off his laptop in his bedroom and went outside to look for Gabby, knowing she was probably lounging near the pool.

He placed a light kiss on her head when he walked over to where she was sitting. Hidden from view, no one would be the wiser of their greeting. She said hello and got up to make him a drink from the terrace bar. Then, she brought it over to him and asked, "How was your day?"

"Fine, if telling our Prime Minister and best friend we're subject to a public health crisis and economic disaster."

Pointing to his cocktail, she said, "You'll probably need more than one of those, let me know when you need a refill."

He smiled and said, "What did you do today?"

"I shopped for the items we needed to stockpile buying a few at the time to not cause alarm, and shopped from several stores on the island. Our freezer and refrigerator are full, and we have plenty of personal items to see us for several months."

"Good job! I've ordered some products to be shipped here too so we should be stocked until this is over. Did you have a chance to talk with Thomason to see what he knows?"

"Yes," she said. "I was surprised he wasn't aware of the Coronavirus. I told him what you said and didn't disclose my source. I mentioned overhearing a health crisis was brewing in China at a cocktail party and he believed me, I think?"

"He thanked me for sharing and said he would investigate and get back with me about whether it was credible or not."

"Can you believe that? One of the top government agencies doesn't know the US will face a health crisis of a pandemic scale?"

"A scary thought for sure," he said.

Reflecting on the conversation with the senator, he knew the government was aware of the serious repercussions with millions being infected and thousands dying. The ones with the inside info were selling off stocks subject to plummet and buying those who would rise during the crisis.

Lulu came out on the terrace and said, "Dinner is ready in the dining room."

They walked inside and called David on the intercom to come down and eat. Lulu's dishes were tasty with Godwin and David having second helpings. After helping Lulu clean the kitchen, they all left for their bedrooms. Godwin smiled at Gabby and knew she'd be down in his bedroom soon.

CHAPTER THIRTY

The Good Samaritans

B EING AN EARLY riser Godwin had the coffee brewing waiting for Gabby to return dressed for the day. After enjoying their morning greeting, he'd head home to begin work on an app to prevent hackers from accessing healthcare-related sites providing information about the virus.

This would be his company's contribution to organizations to halt the deadly virus. Accurate information about the virus was never more important than now. Later, after David awakened, he'd come over to work on projects. With David's creativity, he had no doubt he could develop a software program to run on cell phones to track when you were in the vicinity of someone with the disease. Later, they'd go fishing for dinner and give Lulu the night off and grill on the terrace.

David arrived on his motorcycle and after securing his bike came inside. Godwin had completed the design of his new app and asked David to test it.

David said, "This takes website security up a notch or three. Good to see you've not lost your touch."

"I agree, but we need to run more tests before releasing it. I plan to gift this as our contribution to websites running the latest news about the Coronavirus."

"I'll see if I can hack it using my best nomadic crypto practices," he said.

"Give it your best shot and when you're convinced this app will stop the smart and deft, we'll release it."

"I'll build a pyramid of jangling and run it through the paces," he said.

"Great and when you're ready to take on another project, I want you to plan and develop an app for cell phone users to recognize when they're in the vicinity of someone with the virus. Think, you'd like to create a potentially life-saving app?"

"I'm your hero, for that's right in the wheelhouse of my can-dos."

"Take your time and tweak it and tell me what data you need to access, and I'll pull it for you."

"Yep, we've got this."

They worked in silence most of the day stopping only to make a sandwich for lunch. Godwin remembered the fishing trip to catch some Wahoo for dinner and told David, "We can begin again tomorrow, let's go catch some fish."

David gave him a stunning look for he was deep in the development of the new app, and then said, "You're right, we need a break, I'll meet you at the dock."

They were mentally exhausted and being on the ocean, gave them perspective about their work, and the reality of the world they lived in. They found fish at the navigation coordinates used in the past and reeled in enough fish for dinner and extra to freeze for later in case they couldn't leave the docks.

Working in tandem they quickly cleaned the fish and hosed down the boat, and Godwin said, "Meet you at home in a few minutes."

"You bet."

David pulled his pistol from his saddlebag and placed it on his person before mounting his bike for the short ride home. In the future, he'd remind him not to leave it when parked at the docks. Things could get crazy and someone could steal his weapon.

He drove behind David and as they made Deadman's curve, he remembered what the estate manager said about David, someone was watching his movement.

David had a load on his mind and his social distancing app could benefit the world. He didn't think anyone was gunning for him, but the CIA could make his life difficult if he didn't succumb to their wishes. He needed to tell David about his family's history dating back to his great-grandmother, the Italian Mafia Queen.

His great-grandmother took over as head of the mafia after her husband died. She ran it with the surest fingers along with the vineyard and estate until her death. On David's next trip there he could ask the estate manager about the lineage up until today. His son had one shocker after the other since reaching puberty. He hoped this one would provide benefits for he was due a break.

CHAPTER THIRTY-ONE

Swift Action

D AVID ARRIVED HOME first and dashed to his bedroom and changed into his swimsuit to swim laps in the pool. He said, hello to Gabby for she was lounging on the terrace and typing on her notepad.

"How was your day?" she asked.

"Busy, but we did catch fish for tonight's dinner."

"Sounds yummy, I take it Godwin is right behind you?"

"Yep, he was driving like an old man today. He'll be pulling into the garage soon."

Before the last word came out of his mouth, Godwin walked poolside and said, "It's a good thing I'm not wearing my swimsuit for you deserve a good dunking for calling me an old man."

He laughed and said, "Hello Gabby, I hope you've enjoyed a relaxed day."

"Yes, I have. Lulu and I relaxed and puttered around the house."

"Good, you should do that more often."

Godwin went over and fired up the grill for dinner and went inside to prepare the fish and sides with his special spices.

Gabby breathed easier knowing her secret was safe. In the future, she'd put away her writing tablet before they returned home. She was making progress on her debut romance novel featuring Godwin in a leading role and hoped he'd not recognize himself if he should read it.

They enjoyed a delicious seafood dinner and enjoyed the sunset over the Caribbean. The family had made a pact to not listen to the nightly news for it was too depressing.

She talked to her estate manager in Tuscany daily since the virus infected the country's population and contributed to countless deaths. The manager told her they were locked-in except for shipping wine to their customers and taking care of their workers. Their annual global sales would exceed last year since many residents worldwide were unable to move about as normal.

She reminded him if he needed anything, to call her. He said, "Thank you, but we're good here."

She hoped a vaccine for the virus was forthcoming for she'd love to return to the estate and tour the region and its exciting culture again.

Godwin made the right call about their hunkering down in Barbados. He and David were working on something important for they were acting smug, and they could still fish and relax on the ocean. David would be bored and concerned for their safety if they'd remained in Tuscany especially with the current death toll.

Numerous lives were being saved by Godwin confiding in the Prime Minister about the outbreak months before the island was hit with the deadly virus.

Swift action was taken in Mid-March when the first two cases were confirmed by the Minister of Health and Wellness. A medical facility with over 200 beds was constructed at Harrison Point and a team of intensive care specialists from Cuba arrived and were tested before preparing for the expected wave of infection if it'd creeped through their blockades.

The Prime Minister announced the COVID-19 National Preparedness Plan and later amended it to counteract the spread of the virus with steep consequences for people contravening the order without a reasonable explanation.

Gabby wondered if the new emergency plan would prevent Godwin and David from fishing. Then realized the leadership made plans using the alphabet for last names to buy from fish markets on specific days to feed their citizens.

Godwin was monitoring the CIA source the Italian Mafia had linked him to. He'd hoped with a world-wide pandemic David would be off their radar. But, with him graduating this year, when or if his school reopened, he was ripe for their ongoing watch.

ooooo

He'd completed the MIT registration process and enrolled in the online university courses for a degree in computer science. With his attention to detail, he'd excel in their program for he was already an ace hacker and programmer. This the CIA probably had reconciled with his high school awards. Damn, he wished they'd changed his last name.

He needed to assure David only they were knowledgeable about Deadman's curve. The CIA would come after him about a secret they held and would disclose if he didn't work for them. There were no secrets they uncovered, and he needed to convince David about the impossibility. He'd discuss the rationale with David tomorrow before they began working on their apps.

CHAPTER THIRTY-TWO

Clandestine Affairs

G ABBY DECIDED TO cook dinner and give Lulu a break. She'd had the sauce simmering for hours and hoped it would be as tasty as Godwin made in their early days together. She made a fresh garden salad and the plates were cooling in the refrigerator. In a few minutes, she'd add the spaghetti to the boiling water and when they arrived dinner would be ready.

She hoped they could talk on the terrace while watching the sunset. It was time for them to tell David they were a couple before he discovered it on his own.

David came bursting through the door in a run toward the pool. She wondered what'd happened for usually he managed to walk in the door. Through the window, she saw him coming out of the cabana in his swimsuit. She shook her head, thinking I guess he was ready for a swim.

Godwin entered and kissed her cheek and said, "He completed an app today we believe will help the world distance themselves from Coronavirus carriers and he decided to make it a free download. His adrenaline rush from the excitement needed a healthy release. Why don't we give him some quiet time to work-off his energies?

"Wow, that's a significant milestone for him and I couldn't be prouder. So, that was what you both were being hush-hush about."

"Yep, and we developed a new program to prevent hackers from damaging health-related websites for news about the virus and we're providing free downloads for organizations to update their security."

"You guys have been busy and with good Samaritan offerings. Thank you both for doing your part in making our world a safer place."

She hugged him and he reached down and kissed her lips. "Yes, I'm aware we need to talk to David about us," he said.

"Let's talk tonight after dinner if we get a chance or later in your bedroom after everyone is asleep."

"Yes, we can do that, maybe," he said. "Just keep your robe on until after the conversation."

"Mm, I love my hot-blooded man."

David came in and headed for the kitchen where they were seated. "Congratulations, on your new app," she said. "I'm proud of you and believe you're playing an important role in response to this virus."

David bowed his head and said, "Thank you, I did my best."

She walked over and wrapped her arms around him and said, "Your best will save lives and hopefully provide a solution for reopening businesses for our world to return to a new normal."

Sadness showed in his eyes when he looked up again. She recognized it was personal, he wished he could've saved his mother. She suddenly lost her voice when realizing he'd never forgive her if he learns the truth.

Dinner was ready and everyone filled their plates with Spaghetti and sauce and returned to the table where their salad and drinks were placed. Gabby said the blessing giving thanks for their gifts and gratitude for their home and good health.

Later she and Godwin watched the sunset and discussed how to tell David about them.

"I should talk to him at my home office, and get a feel for his reaction to the news first. What do you think?"

"You're probably right since you spend more time with him than me. I'd love to have his blessings, wouldn't you?"

"Yes, of course. Regardless, in the end, we'll win over his acceptance for our love is eternal."

"Yes, it is," she said.

"For now, we must put on our nightly show of going to our separate bedrooms, until we talk to him about our being a couple."

He kissed her cheek and said, "Let's call it a night, what do you think?"

"Yes, I'll see you after he's gone to sleep."

"I'll be waiting for a beautiful lady."

Gabby rode the elevator to the upstairs suites and saw David in the living area looking at a photo album with pictures of them before the accident. Thomason had been right the lady in the photo looked nothing like she did today. She reached over and touched David's shoulder and he looked up with tears in his eyes. She melted.

He missed his mother, and she couldn't undo the past and put him in danger from one of her pervert adversaries. It was better the secret remains dead, no matter how much she'd like to comfort him with the knowledge his mother lived.

They talked a minute, telling him how much his mother loved him and how proud she'd be of his triumphs today for means to overcome the virus. He smiled and said, "Thank you, I miss her."

"Yes, I know, and I do too."

She left him in the upstairs living room flipping the pages of his life together with his mom and Daniela. She went into her bedroom and changed into her gown and waited until she could slip down the stairs to Godwin's room.

Hours later, she entered Godwin's bedroom and he'd fallen asleep reading his latest crime fiction novel. She lay down beside him and curled up next to him, it was a few hours until sunrise and coffee on the terrace. She tried to sleep to be up early and return to her own bedroom before David stirred.

Godwin was up early and planted a kiss on her lips while she was still sleeping. Their morning routine was cut short for they made love until they feared David would come downstairs.

She went and dressed for the day and returned for coffee on the terrace. David came downstairs and had breakfast at the bar and later came outside where she and Godwin were talking.

"Are you ready to go and let's check on our apps?"

"Sure, David, we'll be on our way in a minute."

"I'll go on over to your place and get started. Come along when you're ready."

"OK, see you in a few. I've almost finished my mug of coffee."

Godwin hadn't got out the door when David called and said, "A CIA agent was sitting outside your house when I arrived. He left his card on the door. What should I do?"

"I'm on the way. Go inside and lock the door until I get there."

Damn, he hoped his makeover passed the test today or his past could sink him and possibly David, too.

Godwin hit his garage door opener and drove in quickly shutting it behind him. He was hoping David could handle the agent and keep to the script they'd discussed if he should be contacted. They should have trademarked his app with a fictitious name for likely that tipped off the CIA to his readiness for clandestine ops.

⟡⟡⟡⟡⟡

"Sooner or later, he'll knock, and you can invite him into the living room. We don't have anything there we're working on and I'll sweep it clean for bugs after he leaves."

"You don't think it'd be better to walk outside and see what he wants?"

"No, for he might try to kidnap you and we'll have a dead body to deal with–his."

"God, I wish I'd used an alias to record this app. My efforts toward a solution for social distancing just backfired."

Godwin handed him a drink from the frig and put the coffee pot on the stove for a fresh brew. The doorbell rang, and David glanced toward him and he nodded. He planned to be seated so his height and bulk wouldn't call attention to him. From behind the tall bar, he could hear the conversation from the foyer.

David opened the door and said, "Yes, how can I help you?"

The agent said, "You're David Jones, are you not?"

"Yes, my name is David, what do you want with me?"

"Our country needs your skills during this unprecedented time to combat this virus. We want you to return to the states and work for us."

David laughed. "You're kidding, right? I haven't completed high school yet and I'd like to pass my finals."

"We can take care of your education and provide a college degree while working with us."

"Well, you're talking to the wrong recruit for I have no interest in working with the CIA or any US government agency."

"That's what we thought you'd say but we have other means for enlisting your help."

"Sounds like blackmail to me, what you got you think will change my mind?"

"You'd first have to agree to work with us, and then we'll open up about your family secrets."

"Wow is that the best you've got. My family secrets are buried six feet underground or incinerated to ashes."

"We can change your mind."

"I think not, and I ask you to leave and never contact me again."

"Have it your way, for now, but you'll need us in the end."

"I don't think so, we're done."

He opened the door for him to leave and waited as he slowly looked around the room before departing.

Godwin's mind was racing trying to figure out what they were up against. The agent didn't see him from where he sat, and David put on a show for him to take back to his superiors.

David closed and locked the front door and said, "I just learned a big lesson. My apps will be listed by another name for I don't want to ever see that clammy-handed man or anyone from that agency."

"You handled the interview well, I'm proud of you but I'm concerned they'll keep coming. The good news is we've got his photo now and can run it on our airport surveillance equipment. I'm still puzzled about how he got into the country with us being on lockdown. He must have entered on a private landing field, let's see where he leaves from."

"Well, at least he didn't get a chance to plant a bug for I didn't allow him further than the foyer."

"Let's sweep the area and the porch quick and be sure."

Godwin was pleased nothing showed up and they were free of bugs.

They went to the computer and watched him travel street by street until he stopped at an abandoned airfield. He'd notify the Prime Minister of its use to eliminate undercover activities on the island.

Godwin remembered he'd promised Gabby to talk with David about their relationship. Maybe before they left for home, but he was thinking David needed to learn about his family's link to the mob. They could provide manpower if something should happen to him. But, would his confiding ancient news add credibility to what the agent suggested?

CHAPTER THIRTY-THREE

Family Secrets

THEY RAN MORE tests on their apps and were relieved no system errors or bugs were found. David was receiving emails from brands about advertising on his app. He declined for he wanted it to serve its purpose only, to alert people when they were near a carrier of the virus. He was thinking of developing a new app for virtual health screening, and ran his idea by Godwin.

"Sounds like it would provide a preliminary health check for the virus and maybe shelter-in-place if they have it. Go ahead and start working on it and if I can help tell me."

"Will do, and thanks."

Godwin smiled and said, "Let's knock off work a little early I need to talk with you about those family secrets."

"Huh, so there are some cloak and dagger in my background?"

"You can say that."

They locked the programs they were working on in the safe, and each grabbed their favorite drink from the frig and sat down at the bar.

"David, you'll find this hard to believe but your great-grandmother was head of the Italian Mob until she passed."

"Nah, now the estate manager, I would believe, but the woman whose portrait hung in the dining hall, I'd say fat chance."

"Why is that?"

"She was beautiful and reminded me of my mother."

"Well, now you know."

"Is Gabby aware of her family's history?"

"Not to my knowledge."

"I won't tell her for she'll want to research the history and perhaps get in harm's way."

"The reason I'm telling you is that the estate manager Dorian is the head now and can be resourceful if you need him."

"I figured you were my back-up. Where are you going?"

"I'll be right beside you; this info is for the future in case of emergencies."

David felt his throat closing and wondered what emergency he should expect where Godwin wouldn't be around.

Godwin put his hand on his shoulder and said, "Are you ready for another secret?"

"It's been a bizarre day so out with it."

"How would you feel about Gabby and me being a couple?"

"Mm, she is a beautiful lady and you're already like family, so why not?"

"Good, I take it we have your blessings?"

"Yes, of course. I want to see you both happy."

"She'll be tickled when you tell her."

"Me?"

"Yes, give her your best wishes for our happiness. She'll probably cry but it'll be from joy and your kindness."

"I can do that."

"Oh, and don't tell her about the CIA agent, she'll have a meltdown for she despises that agency."

"No worries, I kind of expected she'd be upset."

"Well, we can go home now and see what the lady of the house is doing."

"Sounds good to me, I'm ready for a swim and then play online games with my friends."

David saddled his bike and kicked it in gear to head home. Godwin followed from a distance to see if anyone was watching him.

When he arrived, David was already teasing Gabby about their relationship and wishing them the best in the future. He was right; Gabby hugged David and burst into tears of joy. He gently placed his arms around their shoulders and pulled them into his chest, his heart.

ooooo

The next morning, Godwin and David rode to work together after saying goodbye to Gabby. David checked his emails first and was frustrated with the number relating to advertising on his app. He quickly wrote a form letter to reply to some of the leading brands he recognized. Then he noticed an email from the Agent Wither who was in Barbados yesterday. The subject line said, "Your mother is alive!"

He called out to Godwin, "Come look at this email from the CIA."

"Scan it first to double-check for viruses before opening it. They may try to hack into your computer."

David quickly ran a check and said, "My computer is running top speed with the virus protection doing its job."

He opened the email and looked away from Sydney's lifeless body from the car bomb. Godwin quickly covered his mouth in shock after reading the email. The peace he'd felt last night vanished into thin air. The CIA was attacking everything dear to him. Gabby will faint when hearing about this.

He said, "David the burden of proof is on them and they're fishing to learn what you know."

"I believe she was killed with a car bomb by the man I shot on Deadman's curve."

"We both agree they can't know you shot him for we were the only witnesses."

"True."

"Don't respond today to Wither's email. Let's think of a way to end their pursuit of you for their agency."

"I agree for I have no idea what to say."

"Let's run some tests on the programs we have running and leave early to clear our minds.

We can deal with the email tomorrow or another day."

"That sounds, good to me."

They finished their work and rode home quietly together in Godwin's car. Godwin was wondering what David was thinking but gave him space to sort through his thoughts.

On opening the door, they found Gabby busy in the kitchen making dinner. He'd texted her to say they were leaving work early. She recognized a problem and was doing her part to make their day better. Little did she know, but this involved her too. They'd decide the best way to handle the situation tonight and cause David the least heartache. Was it time to be completely honest with David, and break his heart or was the CIA trolling him with lies?

CHAPTER THIRTY-FOUR

Beneath the Lies

DAVID WALKED IN and greeted Gabby and said, "I'm going down to the dock and fish from the shore. How long before dinner will be ready?"

"You'll have an hour before it's cooked."

He turned and smiled with his bottom lip trembling and she wanted to hold him in her arms for him to cry about what was upsetting him. She reached over to comfort him, and he said, "I'll be alright."

"OK, we'll call you when dinner is served."

He kept walking toward the door and her heart sank for something was bad wrong. She didn't think the answers could wait until after dinner.

Godwin knew she would be angry that she wasn't told about the CIA's visit to his home. He was trying to keep her from being upset, at least until the agent showed his hand.

Gabby said, "The tuna noodle casserole is in the oven with the timer set, let's go to your bedroom and talk about what happened today."

He patted the bed for her to sit before disclosing the CIA's pursuit of David. When he finished, she said, "Oh my God, my poor son. How dare they send a picture of my torched body to him?"

He was waiting for her to faint, but her anger kept her conscious. "Gabby, I'm clueless about how they got the picture, but is there a chance one of the paramedics from the accident scene, told them where they took you?"

"I wouldn't know for I was unconscious. I'll call Thomason and tell him what's happening to see if they really have anything or it's just a rouse to pull him into their fold."

"While you're making the call, I'll contact someone who might uncover their plans quietly."

She went to her bedroom to make the call to Thomason and he quickly dialed Dorian in Italy. He brought him up-to-date and asked for his help to verify if the CIA had learned the truth or were fishing.

He said, "You can expect a phone call in a couple of hours."

"Thank you, now I'm confident the CIA was shadowing him in Florence," he said.

He hung up and wondered what Gabby had found out from Thomason. He went into the kitchen to wait and check on dinner. She met him and pointed toward his bedroom for privacy.

She said, "Thomason doesn't think they know anything. The picture was from my accident file proving I'm dead. He's concerned about them stalking David for it could lead to us.

And, yes, he'd determined who you are but it's a secret he'll take to his grave. He said, he knew the whole story and their tactics to control you even to placing a hit on you."

"Well the number of people who know I'm alive just increased to three. But, after what he's done for you, I trust him."

His cell rang, and he said, "I need to take this and said, "Hello."

Dorian said, "The CIA has nothing but they're looking for a trigger to gain his trust. They used the photo of his mother to get his attention. Be watchful when any of you leave home for, they'll be looking for an inside track to David."

"Thanks for the info our country is on lockdown, but we'll still be cautious since they landed illegally here this week."

"Keep me informed and we'll eavesdrop and alert you if David is mentioned."

"We appreciate your back-up," he said. "And, again thanks for the update."

Gabby was listening and when the call ended asked, "Who was that and what did he say?"

"Someone I trust who monitors the CIA's action toward your family. He said, "They have nothing, but we need to be careful of their looking for a way to turn David."

Gabby was sitting on the edge of the bed turning her feet, in tiny slow circles. She stopped and said, "Do you think we should tell David the truth knowing it could jeopardize all of our relationships?"

"I want to say no because the CIA has nothing. The problem is they'll continue watching him and then maybe find us and unravel our secrets. We need a way to get them out of his life."

"Are you saying what I think that he needs a new identity?"

"Yes, and therein lays the problem. We need to tell him the truth for him to make that decision. Don't you think?"

"New identities kept us alive, but I don't think that's the answer for David. He's young and we're heaping a mountain of problems on his head. With most countries in lockdown now from the Coronavirus, we have time to figure out what to do. And, I doubt they can land on the abandoned airfield again."

"You're right," he said. "What about if he doesn't respond to their email and blocks them from future contact?"

"Talk with David and see if he agrees. At least it'll buy us time to make plans and he is a citizen of Barbados since Daniela brought him to the island that may lend support to keep a US agency from harassing him."

"Good idea," he said.

He'd turned off the oven when the buzzer sounded and left the casserole on top of the stove. They quickly began laying out the side dishes on the bar and he went outside to call David for dinner.

David met him on the terrace, and they walked into the kitchen together. "Did you catch any fish," he asked.

"No, but I fed a few," he said.

"Good maybe they'll come back again, and you can snag one."

David said, "Let me wash up and I'll be ready to eat."

"Sure, take your time. We'll wait."

When David returned, he'd washed his tear-stained eyes and was smiling.

They helped their plates and sat at the dining room table to eat. David said, "This tuna casserole isn't bad Gabby maybe you should give Lulu the day off more often."

She laughed and said, "You really think so?"

"Yep, your cooking has improved."

"Thank you, David."

"I was wondering if I could ask you both some questions tonight to help me understand why I'm being targeted by the CIA. I'm sure the new app upped their recruitment schedule, but I was being followed in Italy when we went to Florence before developing it. The spy looked at the beastly men in our group and disappeared.

When reading the email from Wither it reminded me of what I've always known—my mother is alive, although looking at the photo attachment you'd think not. I wanted to ask Daniela about my mom's accident, but she cries at the mention of her name, so I gave up. So, I'm asking you to set the record straight for I want to hear the words from your mouth."

ooooo

Gabby got up and poured a glass of wine and handed Godwin a fresh beer. "David, I'd hoped to never discuss this with you for your own safety. If the people who attempted murder on Sydney realized she'd lived they'd kept coming for her and then after you. And, although the hitman is dead and his employer there are others, she put behind bars who could still order a hit. There was no going back to that life again.

After the accident, Thomason was first on the scene and the exit plan was in place, he sent Sydney to a private burn clinic. Many months passed before she was taken off the ventilator and had numerous skin grafts and facial reconstruction surgery. Several months later he accompanied her from Atlanta to the estate in Italy with a new name. More surgeries were required until returning to Barbados."

She paused and inhaled a deep breath and said, "David I am your mother and I hope you'll forgive me for keeping the secret. And, pray you'll never divulge my identity, not even to Daniela."

"Thank you for telling me the truth. You're being dead never rang true for me and I felt your presence when you arrived from Italy."

David turned and looked at Godwin and asked, "Did you know?"

"No, not until the night before we left for Italy," he said.

Gabby looked at Godwin and said, "Your turn."

David met his eyes and said, "Fill me in."

"David, I have done military ops in the past, and the CIA targeted me for a job with my expertise. They planned to frame me for the murder of someone unless I did their bidding and advised me to never contact your mother again or there'd be consequences.

I, too, have a new identity after realizing they were killing people closest to me to keep me in line and then putting out a hit on me when I didn't. My death in a car accident was faked by a fellow comrade and I've had major surgery to create the man in front of you.

David, I am your father and I recognized it the first time I saw you on the island with your mother when you were young. I've enjoyed our relationship and felt you were safest without knowledge of who I was. But I trust you'll keep this to yourself and forgive both of us for not being forthcoming about our relationship."

Keeping absolute silent David rose and went to Gabby and said, "Welcome to your dream home, mom."

Tears filled Gabby's eyes as she hugged him and said, "Thank you, David, it is our home."

Holding his hands out with the palms up, David went to Godwin and said, "If I'd picked my dad, it would have been you."

Godwin palmed his hands, and said, "If I could have chosen a son, you'd been top pick."

"Now what do we do about the CIA who's masterminding a stake in my life?"

"From your mother's conversation with Thomason the photo they sent was from the accident scene and they haven't uncovered anything. And my source, said the same thing but both warned us to be careful when leaving home so they couldn't learn the truth about your mom and me and open us all to attackers."

"Then what's the next step?"

"Your mother and I think you should not answer the email and block them from future attempts. You're a citizen of Barbados since arriving with Daniela and harassment by a US spy agency won't be tolerated."

"I like your plan and hope it'll work. After tonight I'll not call you mom and dad again, so I won't let it slip accidentally. So, I'm off to bed, but first, goodnight mom and dad."

"Goodnight, son," they said.

Gabby let out the breath she was holding and said, "The truth stings for a while, but it will set you free, and I think that's what happened tonight. We are free at last my love to fight as *one* for our family."

The End

FROM THE AUTHOR, CAROLYN BOWEN

Thank you for reading the Sydney Jones Series, Book 3 *One*. Stay connected for details about special offers and giveaways to gift your friends and family.

Word of mouth is crucial for any author to succeed. If you've enjoyed the novel, please consider leaving a review, even if it is only a line or two; it would make all the difference and I would appreciate it very much.

Follow me on my website for the latest news about my new releases and fun social promotions. As always, I appreciate you!

Carolyn Bowen, Author—cmbowenauthor.com

Made in the USA
Columbia, SC
16 January 2021

30098779R00140